PRINCE(ISH) AND THE PEACE

CAROLYN LAROCHE

CHAPTER ONE

The thumping of the bass exactly matched time with the thumping in his head. For the hundredth time that night, Patrick wondered why he'd agreed to this weekend. His buddy changed girls like most men changed their jeans. The thought that Devin might actually marry someone still felt like a joke to him.

The bachelor's weekend in Virginia Beach had turned into a get laid quest that Patrick had absolutely no interest in. He'd thought they'd drink beer, eat greasy food and maybe smoke a good cigar or two. Devin had two weeks until his wedding and at the rate this weekend had been going, he probably wouldn't even make it to the altar. Rebecca deserved way better than his childhood friend—he loved Devin like a brother but that didn't change facts. Even in middle school, Devin's charm had gotten him anything he wanted. He'd only gotten better—and more egotistical—with age.

Patrick glanced around the crowded bar only to find Devin and his twin brother Derek seated at a table with women that definitely weren't theirs perched on their laps. Devin caught him looking as he nibbled at his date's ear lobe and waved him over, pointing to a woman sitting by herself. The pouty brunette wore way too much make up and definitely not enough clothes.

He shook his head slightly. Uh-uh, no way. There wasn't enough alcohol in the bar that would make him want any part of that adventure. If nothing else, he's always preferred the natural look.

Digging into his pocket, he pulled his cell phone out and waved it at Devin then pointed to the door. He had no one to call and his phone hadn't rung in hours but Devin would automatically assume a work call had come in since Patrick never really stopped working. He had to get the hell out of that bar before he lost his mind or Devin lost something else and the work angle always played well.

Without registering his friend's response, Patrick headed to the back hall where the bathrooms were. He'd seen an exit there that the employees used to step out for smoke breaks. If he played his cards right, he could sneak out the back way and return to his hotel room before the other guys even missed him. Not that Patrick was the top thought in their minds anyway. No, he was fairly certain they weren't thinking much with their brains at the moment.

As soon as he stepped into the hallway, the sound level dropped in half. He followed the dark walkway to the exit sign that glowed from its spot high on the wall and pushed at the cold steel handle. The door slipped open and Patrick stepped outside, breathing in the cool, ocean air. His blood pressure instantly dropped about twenty points. Despite the fall temperatures, he could still smell the saltiness of the sea, something he'd always found cathartic, and the number one reason he'd agreed to this trip. He should have just stayed home in Raleigh and done the big sale with his parents but the whole Prince of Sleep thing had gotten old, fast.

Patrick leaned against the brightly painted wall of the building and opened the internet browser on his cell phone. Typing in a quick search for local restaurants, he waited while the list loaded. There had to be someplace quiet nearby where he could get a drink and something to eat before heading to his hotel room. He scrolled through the options, settling on a small craft beer establishment a couple blocks past the hotel.

Sticking his phone in his pocket, Patrick headed toward the front of the building. A man's desperate voice carried over the light breeze, catching his attention, before it disappeared. He stopped walking and turned to look into the dark alley. He couldn't see or hear anything until the sound of a man whimpering broke the silence.

"I told you! I won't testify! I swear it!"

A second, gruff voice spoke next. "Loose ends, man. The boss don't like no loose ends."

Patrick, moving carefully, followed the sound of the conversation that appeared to come from the opposite end of the space.

"Why do you think I escaped?" Patrick could hear the fear in the man's voice. "Then I found *you*, remember? Why would I do that if I were a rat?"

Patrick continued to move slowly, his phone in his hand. He stopped walking so he could dial nine one one.

"Sorry, man. Boss told me too." There wasn't an ounce of apology in his words.

Patrick hit send on the call. A gunshot sounded. Then another in close succession. He dropped his phone with a loud clatter.

"Who's there?" Footsteps pounded against the pavement, stopping when he spotted Patrick. "What the hell you doin' here?"

Patrick threw his hands in the air as the other man waved his pistol in the space between them. "I —I just came out to make a call."

"Shit!" The man kicked at Patrick's phone, the emergency number clearly displayed on the screen. "Another damn loose end."

He stepped back again, until his heel hit the base of a dumpster. "I won't say anything to anyone."

The man stepped forward, gun pointed at Patrick and a sneer twisting his lips. "That's not how this works."

"Please. Just walk away. I didn't see anything and I don't know anything. I just want to go back to my hotel and go to bed." Patrick's pleas sounded pathetic, even to him.

"I can't leave a loose end. Boss's orders."

"Don't tell the boss?" As soon as the words left his mouth, Patrick regretted them.

A tiny, evil smile turned up the corner of the man's lips as he moved a little closer. "I got a better idea."

Knowing exactly what the man had in mind, Patrick took another backward step. Not that it mattered, he was now backed up to the brick wall of the building.

A bright flash lit up the night. White hot pain seared through him as the bullet struck his shoulder. The force of it jerked his entire body, his head smacking against the corner of the dumpster. The resounding crack of skull on steel nearly drowned out the man's footsteps as he ran out of the alley. Knees buckling, Patrick crumpled to the cold ground, his head hitting a hard surface for the second time.

"I told you I wouldn't say anything," he

murmured as his eyes closed and the world slipped slowly into darkness.

"Is he dead?"

Sylvia nudged the body on the ground with the toe of her boot, avoiding the bloody spots. Her boots were too nice to be wearing around a DOA. They were just supposed to take her from Raleigh to New York as she transported a witness in a big time, interstate trafficking case. She hadn't expected to be chasing down said witness in the middle of the night in Virginia Beach because the ass gave her the slip at a rest stop.

She leaned down to peer at the motionless body. "Hey, Mack." She waved her partner over. "Looks like the guy took a bullet and a whack to the head."

Mack pulled the toothpick out of his mouth that he'd been chewing on since dinner and looked around the alley. "Poor son of a bitch. I bet he never knew what hit him."

Sylvia stood up, smoothing her palms over the front of her jeans. "I kinda feel bad for the guy."

Something grabbed her ankle. Sylvia screamed, kicking at it. "It's got me! Ewww! Rats! Get it off me!" She danced in a circle, kicking her foot out and hitting the dead guy in the ribs.

"Ouch! Hey, I'm not dead down here."

Sylvia stopped jumping and looked down at the man on the ground, his eyes closed and his body still. "Did you hear that?" she asked Mack.

"Hear what?" Mack had his phone in his hand, typing a text.

"The dead guy talked."

"I'm not dead." The man on the ground moaned and grabbed her ankle again. "Don't kick me anymore. It hurts."

Mack squatted down and held his palm over the man's nose. "I'll be a son of a monkey. He's *alive*."

"That's what I'm trying to tell you." The man opened one eye and looked at them. "What happened? Everything hurts."

Sylvia clapped a hand to her mouth. "Damn it, man. I'm sorry."

"Just stop." His eye closed again as he let out a sigh/moan combination.

Sylvia waved to a couple of medics. "Hey, y'all, bring the stretcher over here."

"This here sorry sack is still breathin'!" Mack called out.

Twice her age and as old school as they come, Gene "Mack" McCoy, could be real rough around the edges. The agency had talked retirement with him many times but, he was a kick ass Marshal and had saved her butt more than a time or two so she refused to work with anyone else. This trip was supposed to be his last gig for the agency before he retired at the end of the week.

Two medics appeared with a stretcher and a gear bag. "Let us in," a female medic said, elbowing past Sylvia and Mack.

"He's a lot luckier than the other son of a bitch." Mack waved toward the end of the alley where their witness lay.

Sylvia swung an arm around the shoulders of her partner as they walked over to the crime scene. "Guess you're not retiring on Friday after all. Too bad."

"Oh no, little girl. I've given the agency thirty years of my life. I'm done."

"You're gonna leave me to handle this whole mess myself?" Sylvia squatted and pulled the man's wallet and cell phone from his pocket. "So much for witness protection. This sorry sap could have had a whole new life courtesy of the U.S Department of Justice. Instead, he went and got himself murdered."

Mack's phone chimed, indicating an incoming text message. He read the message then grinned at Sylvia.

Sylvia used her own cell phone to take a few photographs of the victim. "What's so amusing?"

Mack chuckled and handed her his phone. "You're gonna love this."

She took the phone and read the message. "Oh, hell no!"

The message, from their boss Tom Carruthers read *Tell SF she's on guard duty. He's our witness now and she can't let him out of her sight.*

"I'm not babysitting. No way. All I brought was a change of clothes. He could be in the hospital for days. Or *weeks*." Sylvia kicked at an empty beer can. It bounced, spilling its contents on her boot. Apparently, it wasn't actually empty. "I knew I should have stayed in North Carolina."

Mack shrugged. "He's an eye witness to the murder of our witness. Someone's got to keep an eye on him and I've got one foot out the retirement door." He pointed toward the ambulance. "You better get moving, they're about to pull out."

"Crap! Fine. But you owe me!" Sylvia jogged toward the ambulance, stopping once to turn around. "Steak dinner. I *will* collect when this over!"

Mack gave her a salute before turning his attention to the medical examiner that had just arrived.

Sylvia reached the ambulance and stopped, bending over to catch her breath.

"You might need this stretcher more than me."

Sylvia straightened and peered into the back of the vehicle to find the shooting victim smiling at her. "Sorry about earlier, um, what did you say your name is?"

He pointed to a name tag stuck to his sweater. "Prince Patrick, apparently."

One of the EMT's appeared at her side. "We need to head out, ma'am."

"I'm going with you." She pulled her ID from her pocket and showed it to the young man. "This man may have witnessed the murder of a man in protective custody."

The EMT motioned to the inside of the truck. "Hop on in but you're wasting your time."

"Why?" Sylvia narrowed her eyes at the man.

He walked a few feet away and motioned for Sylvia to follow. "Poor sap can't remember anything."

"Nothing?" She looked over at the man in the bed and then back to the EMT. "He just told me his name."

"Prince Patrick?"

She nodded. "Yeah."

"Dude's wearing a paper sticker that says Prince Patrick on it. It's the only identification he's got."

Sylvia rolled her eyes. "Well, that's just flipping wonderful."

"Trauma induced amnesia is usually very short term. His head took a good whack and he's been shot. He's lucky to be alive, if you ask me."

"The wound didn't look life threatening."

He shook his head. "It's not the wounds I'm talking about. Someone tried to kill him. Based on the other body at the scene, I'm thinking his injury was a fluke. It should have been fatal."

"You know your stuff." She stuck out her hand. "Name's Sylvia Fairfax, US Marshal Service."

The EMT shook it. "James Boyd. My dad's been on the job my whole life. Dinner time conversations were, shall we say, unique?"

Sylvia chuckled. "I know what you mean. Let's get Prince Patrick to the hospital, shall we? With any luck, his memory will come back with some medical treatment."

James led the way, waiting until Sylvia climbed in and then pulled the doors closed behind them. This was going to be a very long night.

CHAPTER TWO

She settled on one of the bench seats and held her badge out. "So, Prince Patrick, I'm Agent Fairfax with the U.S. Marshal Service. Can you tell me what happened tonight?"

"I was shot and I guess I hit my head."

"Do you remember anything about the person who shot you?"

Patrick winced as James lifted his wrist to check his pulse. "Nope."

"Do you have any idea why you were in that alley?"

He let his eyes close as a sigh escaped his lips. "I wish I did."

Sylvia looked at James who nodded and made the sign for sleep, pretending to rest his head on his hands. She nodded and sat back against the wall of the ambulance. Sleep could help his memory come back.

The ride was short and fast. In less than five minutes they pulled up to the emergency room entrance. A team of medical staff met them as the doors to the truck opened.

"Talk to me," one of the nurses said. To the others she said, "Get him in a room and prep him for surgery."

"Male, single gunshot wound to the shoulder and a head injury, cause undetermined. Vitals are decent. BP 128/86, pulse 55."

"Name?"

"Prince Patrick," Sylvia said. James chuckled and the other staff gave her an odd look.

"Is Prince his last name?" the nurse asked.

Sylvia shrugged. "Your guess is as good as mine. He has no identification or cell phone on him and his memory is completely gone. He has a sticker on his shirt that says Prince Patrick."

"He might need surgery. We'll figure out who he is later." The nurse turned and strode toward the doors, Sylvia and James close on her heel.

"Where are you going?" the nurse asked Sylvia as she pulled open one of the doors.

"That man is in protective custody. He's not supposed to be out of my sight."

"And I need my bed back," James said.

The nurse rolled her eyes at him. "I wasn't asking

you. Just go. You know procedure." She turned to Sylvia, tapping her pen to the clipboard she carried. "But you, well, you can't just hang out in the operating room."

Sylvia rested her hand on the butt of the pistol she wore on her hip. "I have a job to do."

Nurse Jodie, Sylvia could see her name tag now, glanced at her hip and then back up. "You gonna shoot me, officer?"

"I'm an agent of the federal government, not an officer and, no, I don't plan to shoot you at the moment. However, your patient—and my witness— is in danger. I need to be able to protect him."

"What exactly did he get himself mixed up in?" James asked, pushing the stretcher past them and loading it into the ambulance.

"We're still trying to figure that out but it's nothing good. Not based on the other body at the scene. Someone known to us for way too many reasons."

Jodie threw her hands in the air and let out a frustrated sigh. "Fine. If he needs surgery, you can stand outside the OR door and watch him through the window. That's the best I can do."

Sylvia gave her a curt nod. "Works for me. For now."

Jodie made a note on the chart she carried on a clipboard. "The whole thing is just ridiculous. What could happen to him in the OR? You should go get something to eat. Take advantage of the fact that we have him in a safe space."

She'd never admit it to the nurse but Jodie had a point. She *was* hungry, and could use a trip to the ladies' room. "Just show me where he is for now and I'll decide how secure he is when I see the operating room."

Jodie shook her head and made another notation on her chart. "Fair enough, I suppose. Follow me."

The other woman led the way down a dim hall to a curtained space at the back of the emergency department.

Sylvia stepped into the space to find her witness asleep. She settled in the chair by the bed and pulled out her phone. Swiping a message open from Mack she growled when she saw the picture of the juicy steak dinner he sent her.

"Imbecile," she said, sticking her tongue out at her phone.

"You or the phone?"

Sylvia looked up so see Patrick watching her through the loose waves that had fallen across his forehead, a teasing glint mixed with the obvious pain in his eyes. "What?

"Are you calling yourself an imbecile? Or your phone?"

Resisting the sudden urge to smooth that hair back from his eyes, she shoved the phone in her jacket pocket and frowned. "I thought you were sleeping. Has your memory come back yet?"

"I'm doing okay, thanks for asking." Patrick lifted his uninjured arm and covered his eyes with it. "And, no, it hasn't."

Sylvia frowned. The longer it took for him to remember, the longer she'd be stuck babysitting.

"Good evening, Mr. Prince." A tall man wearing scrubs and wool socks with a pair of Birkenstocks stepped into the space. He turned to Sylvia, hand extended. "I'm Dr. Rivers. Are you Mrs. Prince?"

"No!" Sylvia jumped to her feet, pulling her credentials from her pocket. "I'm US Marshal Sylvia Fairfax. This is my witness. His name isn't Mr. Prince."

Looking amused, Dr. Rivers studied the chart, his brow furrowing as he read. "That's what it says here."

"He's got amnesia or something. Says he can't remember anything." She pointed toward Patrick's chest. "His name tag says, Prince Patrick, but he has no idea what it means."

"Hello." Patrick waved his uninjured arm. "I'm right here, people. Stop talking about me like I'm dead or something, just because I don't remember who I am."

"I'm so sorry, sir." Dr. Rivers walked over to the bed. "Let's take a look at your injuries."

Patrick leaned forward slightly so the doctor could examine the wound on his head. He checked

Patrick's eyes and then examined the shoulder wound. Sylvia watched in silence as Patrick winced with each probe of the doctor's fingers.

"So, you definitely have a concussion. Your left pupil isn't reactive to light the way we'd like it to be. Your shoulder wound, however, is a very clean, through and through shot. The bleeding has all but stopped. I'm going to order a CT and an MRI to scan for any internal damages but I don't think you'll need surgery, just some stitches and a round of heavy duty antibiotics. You'll be out of here in two or three days, tops."

"Two or three days!" Sylvia couldn't stop the words. She clapped a hand over her mouth.

Dr. Rivers nodded as made a couple of notations in the computer he'd logged into. "I'm afraid so, Miss. Don't worry though, he should be absolutely fine."

Sylvia paced the tiny space. Two steps to the left and two steps to the right. "It's not that. This was supposed to be a quick overnight trip."

"You can just go on about your business. I'm sure they will figure out who I am eventually."

She stopped moving and glared at the man in the bed. "You *are* my business. I can't just leave the only person that witnessed the death of a high value government asset."

"High value government asset? Lady, you found me in an alley wearing a sticker that claims I'm a prince with no money, no identification, and no memory. I'm no value to anyone."

Propping a hand on her hip, Sylvia narrowed her eyes at him. "Not *you*. The man you saw get shot. He's our asset. I have no idea who you are."

Patrick reached over and wrapped his fingers around her wrist. A shot of pure energy passed between them, warming Sylvia in places that had been dormant way too long. "That makes two of us, sister."

The electricity that arched between them when he grabbed Sylvia's wrist could have lit up the entire city. The shock of it caused a slight groan to escape his lips. He really hoped she thought it was because of one of his injuries.

The doctor looked from Patrick to Sylvia and back again, his expression tinted with a slight smile. "I'll have the nurse set things up and then I will be back to sew you up. In the meantime, I'll schedule those tests and see about getting you admitted."

"Thanks, doc."

Dr. Rivers left the space. Patrick never looked away from Sylvia's dark green eyes. The color of emeralds and perfect accent to her dark hair, those eyes would have made him forget everything, if he hadn't already.

Sylvia glanced down at his hand, still holding on to her. "You can let go. I'm not leaving and, unfortunately, neither are you."

"Good evening, Mr. Prince." The curtain parted and an older woman wearing green scrubs and her hair in a tight knot as the base of her head stepped in to the space, pushing a small cart. "We're gonna get you sewn up and then set you up with deluxe accommodations upstairs for the next few days."

"Dr. Rivers said two days. You think it will be longer?" She tugged at her arm as she spoke. Patrick reluctantly let go of Sylvia's wrist and she stepped quickly away from the bed, out of his reach.

The nurse shrugged. "That decision is above my pay grade. But, either way, sweetie, your man will be as good as new once Dr. Rivers is done. He's the best there is in this department. Actually, the entire hospital, if you ask me."

"He is not my *man*. He's my witness." Sylvia flashed her badge again, quick to define their relationship.

Not that they had a relationship. He didn't even know her. Heck, at the moment he didn't even know himself. Something about Marshal Sylvia Fairfax intrigued him though.

Not that it mattered. He could have a wife somewhere. He looked down at his left hand. No ring. No ring tan. Okay, so probably not married. Maybe a girlfriend? He shifted on the annoyingly uncomfortable mattress.

"This sucks." He shifted again.

Sylvia scowled. "Not exactly a dream date for me either."

"I meant this bed. I can feel every metal bar through the mattress."

She chuckled. "This isn't the Hyatt. Maybe your name tag should have read *Princess*. Can you feel the tiny pea poking at you?"

"Don't quit your day job. Comedy is not your talent." He moved one more time. Pain shot down his arm and he moaned. "I think the pain meds are wearing off."

The nurse patted his leg. "Not to worry young man, I'm about to fix that right now." Using a large syringe, she injected some liquid pain medicine into his IV. "In about three seconds you won't feel a thing."

In his head, Patrick counted to three. The room became hazy. Sylvia grew a second head and he could have sworn he saw birdies circling his own head.

"Ohhhh, wowwww." Patrick let his eyelids close slightly to block out the sharp glare of the overhead lights. "Is this what it feels like?"

"What feels like?" Sylvia leaned over and looked down at him.

Patrick reached up to touch her face and missed.

There were now three Sylvia's staring at him, grinning. "Drugs."

The nurse laughed. "He's on a major trip right now. In a few more minutes he'll fall asleep and won't feel a thing."

Patrick nodded. At least he tried to. His head felt like it weighed a thousand pounds. "I *am* kinda tired."

"We ready to stitch up that wound and get you down to the imaging department?" Dr. Rivers stepped into the tiny room, this time wearing a white coat and pulling on some gloves.

"Sure thing, doc." His words sounded odd to his own ears. Like the letters had all run together.

"He's high as a damn kite, Dr. Rivers." Sylvia laughed. "I'll get out of the way now."

Patrick reached out and grabbed her hand. "Stay. Please."

Sylvia gave him a confused look. "Why?"

"I don't like needles." His head lolled to the side, his tongue feeling two sizes too big for his mouth. Air refused to get into his lungs. Patrick gasped, trying to suck in oxygen.

"Um, doctor, I think something's wrong. He can't breathe. And his lips are turning blue."

Doctor Rivers looked up from his surgical supplies. "What do you—oh wow! He's having an anaphylactic reaction to the pain medicine. Nurse! I need epi, *right now!*"

The tighter his throat felt, the tighter he

squeezed Sylvia's hand. Black spots danced before his eyes, taunting him with complete darkness.

When he next opened his eyes, sunlight streamed through the partially opened curtains on the lone window in the tiny room. The smell of disinfectant lingered with something even less appealing, like vomit.

"Where am I?" The pain it caused when he spoke, cut right through him.

"Virginia Beach General Hospital."

Patrick turned his head to the side and caught sight of the stunning brunette sitting beside him, her emerald eyes filled with concern. "You nearly died. Twice now, actually."

"Agent Fairfax. Right. I forgot, someone tried to kill me and I don't know who I am." He tugged at a loose thread of the blanket that covered him.

Sylvia reached over and placed her hand over his. The simple touch fired off some not so simple reactions in his sore body. "You had an allergic reaction to the pain medicine they gave you in the emergency room."

Patrick frowned. "I don't have any allergies. At least, I didn't think I did. But, who knows."

She squeezed his hand lightly before pulling away. "We will figure out who you are, I promise."

"You don't care if I ever figure out who I am." He looked toward the window, not meeting her gaze.

"All you're worried about is me remembering who killed your really important witness."

"That's not true." He heard the words but her tone told a different story. She wanted to be done with the whole mess and head back to wherever she'd come from. Knowing this bothered him more than it should have since he really wanted to be done with the whole thing too.

He slammed his fist against the air-filled mattress. "Why can't I remember? And who thought this poor excuse for a mattress was a good idea?"

Sylvia chuckled. "You're a real prima-donna when it comes to your beds, aren't you?"

He looked at her, one eyebrow raised. "What are you talking about?"

"You complained about the gurney in the ER and now you're complaining about this perfectly good air mattress."

"So, what? I've been shot. Is it too much to ask to *not* feel every steel bar in the bed frame?"

Sylvia rolled her eyes. "Whatever." She grabbed a small notebook and pen from her bag. "Maybe we should concentrate on what we do know. It might help your memory come back."

Patrick leaned into the pillow and stared up at the ceiling. "I know someone shot me. I don't know why but it likely had something to do with the other dead guy."

He watched as Sylvia made a note on her paper.

Two little lines formed in between her eyes as she focused on whatever thought she needed to process.

She looked up from her notes. "We also know that you aren't from around here."

"How do you know that?" he asked.

"If things were familiar to you it would jog your memory."

He could accept that. "Okay, so I'm probably not a local."

"Not a local but definitely royalty, *Prince* Patrick." She winked at him, a sparkle lighting her emerald eyes that stoked a tiny fire in his sore body.

Closing his eyes against both the burn and the pain, he grunted. "I know for a fact that I'm not royal. I have no idea what that means but it has to be some kind of joke."

"We also know that you have little to no sense of humor."

Patrick opened his eyes and looked at her. "I've been shot, have a concussion, and nearly died from an allergic reaction in less than ten hours. I don't feel much like laughing."

He grabbed the control for the bed and pushed the button to get in to a sitting position and swung his legs to the side. Someone had set a walker beside his bed. He gripped the handles and summoned all his energy to get to his feet.

"Where are you going?" Sylvia jumped up and started to move toward him.

"I'm just going to the bathroom. I promise not to make a break for it."

She stepped back, waving a hand to motion him through. "I'll be right here, anxiously awaiting your return, sir."

Patrick ignored the snarky comment and focused on remaining upright as he took one step and then another. Once he was certain he wouldn't fall flat on his face, he slowly moved toward the small bathroom. Working the walker and dragging the IV pole along took forever. He felt Sylvia's gaze on his back, his skin heating as a fleeting image of her hands on the bare skin skittered through his mind.

"You're a real mess, man," he muttered as he shuffled in to the bathroom, using his pole for support.

Closing the door behind him, he stared in to the mirror. Dried blood ran in a dark shadow along his hair line. He'd need to ask about showering. His hair had to be full of blood and dirt from the ground in the alley. He cringed at the thought of it. Reaching up, he pressed his fingertips to a bruise on his cheekbone, directly under his eye. A quick image flashed through his head. The memory of someone, he couldn't see who, holding a gun aimed at him. The image disappeared as quickly as it had appeared.

He pushed the pole away and gripped the sides of the sink, moving in close enough to the mirror he could see the gold flecks in his blue eyes but couldn't see a single thing that told him who he really was.

A tiny little part of him whispered deep in his brain that it might be okay if it took a day or two for his memory to come back. Marshal Sylvia intrigued him, making him as curious about her as himself.

A loud crash sounded from the other side of the door, followed by a long string of curses. Patrick chuckled. Sylvia's southern drawl she worked so hard to hide slipped out and accented each of the words, making them sound prettier than they were.

CHAPTER THREE

Sylvia watched as Patrick made his way to the bathroom, slightly grateful that it took so long. It gave her the chance to study the way his muscles tensed across his back as he moved. A man built like that took care of himself, probably worked out regularly. Add that to the list of things they knew about the mystery that was *Prince Patrick*.

She walked over to the window and stared down at the busy road that ran in front of the hospital. The cool glass fogged up from her breaths. The last time she'd stood at a window in a hospital room, it was to say goodbye to the love of her life.

Patrick reminded her of Wyatt in a lot of ways. The intensity in his stare, the kind that seemed to penetrate straight to her soul. Wyatt had left a huge hole in her heart and life. Her job had become the salve to her pain and sitting still this long in a place that carried too many memories only served to deepen that wound.

Sylvia sighed and turned away from the window.

Eventually he would be missed enough by *someone*. With any luck at all, his memory would come back first and they'd be able to get the information they need from him.

Her phone buzzed in her bag. As she stepped over to the chair, the heel of her boot caught on a cord turning her ankle and she flew forward, crashing into the bedside table which then slammed into the wall.

A long string of all her favorite cuss words fell from her lips, an image of her southern belle mama listening in horror popping up, as she slammed her arm on the rolling table. She straightened, rubbing her forearm and stretching the ankle that had twisted. "Just what I need."

Sylvia grabbed her phone from her bag and sat down on the edge of the bed, swinging her injured leg up onto the mattress. Leaning back against the raised bed she swiped the screen to see a text from Mack.

Headed back to Raleigh.

She quickly typed her response. *I hope your car runs out of gas in Camden County and you have to walk ten miles.*

Mack's reply came quickly. *I can already hear the banjos. See you on the other side of the river.*

I hope you fall in that river and the gators pick your bones clean. Sylvia hit send then turned off her phone. Sighing, she closed her eyes against the tears that threatened. Mack got to go home and she got to babysit.

Yay.

Shifting on to her side, she lifted her other leg on to the bed. She just needed a couple of minutes to rest while Patrick used the bathroom. With a bit of luck, he'd be in there awhile. She yawned. Patrick had been right about one thing. She could feel every single metal bar of the frame.

When she opened her eyes again, the room was considerably darker. She looked toward the window and discovered the blinds had been drawn. Little slivers of orange evening light cut through the plastic blades.

Sylvia tried to roll over but something stopped her. Pushing herself into a sitting position she looked over at the bed and found Patrick laying there, sound asleep, one leg dangling off the side.

Crap! How long had she been asleep?

Glancing at her phone, Sylvia sucked in a breath. Over three hours had passed. Jumping off the bed, she cursed once more as pain shot through her. Damn it, she forgot about her ankle.

"Are you okay?" Patrick asked, his voice thick with sleep.

"You slept with me." She turned on him, hands on her hips.

He opened one eye and peered out at her under impossibly long eyelashes. "This is my bed. You slept with me."

"Semantics." She dropped into the chair, her ankle giving up on her. "You should have just woken me up."

"You looked so peaceful." He smiled. "And when you sleep, you don't talk."

Sylvia scowled. "You're a real charmer."

"I had another motive as well. With both of us on the bed, it balanced the air mattress and made it harder to feel the frame."

A knock sounded at the door, as it pushed open and a short, older man with a full white beard that could have rivaled Santa Claus entered the room. He carried a small tablet computer. "Good afternoon, I'm Doctor Wallis."

"Hey, doc." Patrick gave him a little salute. "Am I breaking out of the joint?"

Doctor Wallis chuckled. Sylvia couldn't help but notice that his belly jiggled when he did. Sort of like a bowl full of jelly. She hid a smile.

"Not tonight, young man. You get one more night's stay in these deluxe accommodations. That was a pretty intense reaction you had in the E.R."

"Everyone keeps telling me that. I don't remember a thing. Not even my own name, it would seem." Patrick frowned and Sylvia heard the sadness in his voice.

"More than likely it was intensified by the other traumas." The doctor set his computer down on a counter and walked over to the bed. "Let's have a look, son." Reaching up to a switch on the wall, he turned on an overhead light and used a tongue depressor to part Patrick's hair. "That's a hefty lump you have. How's your head feel?"

Patrick shrugged. "A little achy, I guess."

The doctor nodded as he moved to the bandages on Patrick's shoulders. He pulled the front one open first then the one on the back side of his shoulder. "The concussion is basically a bruise to your brain. You're going to feel it for a bit. How's your eyesight? Any double vision? Floating spots?"

"Not really. If I stand or sit too fast, it takes a minute to adjust but that's it."

Doctor Wallis nodded again. "That sounds about right. These wounds actually look really good. You are a very lucky man."

"I'm not feeling so lucky."

"Yeah, poor guy can't even remember his name," Sylvia said. "Is the concussion responsible for that?"

"Could be." The doctor ran his fingers through his white beard. "Could also be a defense mechanism protecting his brain from the traumatic experience of someone attempting to murder him."

She sighed. This was not what she wanted to

hear. "How long until it comes back? I need to get back to Raleigh, sooner rather than later."

"It's hard to say. You can take him home tomorrow to Raleigh. Just make sure he sees his own doctor for follow up."

Sylvia nodded once. "Once we figure out who he is, where he's from, and who his doctor is, we'll be sure to do that."

"Well, good luck with all of that." Doctor Wallis closed his little laptop and smiled at Patrick. "I'll be back in the morning. As long as you have an uneventful night, I'll release you."

"Thanks, Doc." Patrick gave a little wave then covered his eyes with his uninjured arm. When they were alone, Patrick sighed, the loud breath laced with frustration. "Where do I go?"

"What?" Sylvia asked, lifting her leg with the injured ankle up and resting it on the bed.

"Where do I go? I'm being released in the morning but I have nowhere to go."

"*We* are going to check in to a seedy motel down by the beach and stay incognito until you remember you who are."

"You've seen way too many episodes of *Super-natural*."

She laughed. "What makes you say that?"

Patrick turned his head and peered out at here under his arm. "The Winchesters always stay in seedy motels. The seedier the better."

"For your information, the Marshal service likes them too. Less chance of standing out in a crowd. But, yeah, I'm a fan of the show too."

"Dean or Sam?" Patrick asked.

Sylvia relaxed in to the chair, with a happy exhale of air. "Neither."

Patrick sat up in his bed. "Now, I call bull shit on that one. Every woman in the world is either Team Dean or Team Sam."

She shrugged. "Sam's too whiny and Dean's too *the world is ending and I'm the only one who can save it.* Personally? I'm a Crowley fan. Now that dude is bad ass."

Patrick laughed. "He's the King of Hell! He's just bad."

"You say tomato, I say tomahto."

"I'm surprised you don't go for Castiel." Patrick relaxed against the pillow again but didn't cover his eyes this time. "You seem like a gal that would go for the strong, simple type."

Sylvia leaned forward in her chain. "Are you calling the *angel* Castiel simple? Oh yee, of no biblical training, how wrong you are. He could kill you with a snap of his fingers."

"You do realize we are talking about a fictional character on a fictional television show, right?" The amusement in his voice annoyed the crap out of her.

"I'm done with this conversation." Sylvia waved

her hand in dismissal. "I'm hungry. How do I call room service in this joint?"

"You haven't eaten since yesterday, have you?" Patrick sounded concerned but she waved it away. "You don't have to babysit me. It's not like I have anywhere to go."

"My job is to protect you, not guard you. You're not under arrest. However, we *do* believe your life is in danger."

"So, you have to starve? Go to the cafeteria. What could happen to me locked up in here?"

Sylvia sighed. "You'd be surprised."

Her stomach chose that very moment to let out a loud protest to its hunger. Patrick laughed as her face heated with embarrassment. He waved toward the door. "Go. Feed the demon. I'll be fine."

She looked around the small space and then at the door. There was no direct line of sight from the hallway to the bed. If she grabbed some food and brought it back to Patrick's room, she'd be gone ten minutes, tops. Five if she moved fast. Strike that. Her sore ankle might make it fifteen. Every ounce of her soul said not to go, she had a job to do. Her stomach growled again, sending out another loud warning.

"Fine. I'll be back in a flash though. Don't do anything crazy while I'm gone."

Patrick mock saluted. "Yes, ma'am."

Sylvia slowly stood, testing her sore ankle gently.

When it appeared to hold her weight with the minimum amount of discomfort, she picked up her bag and left the room.

The second Sylvia left the room, it felt cold and empty. Patrick hated to admit it to himself but she'd been growing on him. She had the posture of a debutante and the grace of a rhinoceros. She tried to hide her injury but he knew that crash he'd heard had been all Sylvia. Her quick wit and dry sense of humor appeared to complement his own quite well. Add that to the list of things he knew about himself.

A knock on the door interrupted his thoughts of those sharp green eyes that seemed to pierce him to his soul.

"Come in."

The door opened and the scent of fresh coffee and a hot meal filled his little room. "I've brought you dinner, sir."

A tall, thin woman dressed in green scrubs carried a tray in and set it on the rolling bedside table.

"Thank you so much. I'm starving. And, I have no idea how long it's been since I've had coffee."

She gave him a sweet smile. "It's hospital food for sure. Bland as can be. I put some salt, pepper, and hot sauce on the tray for you. Anyone under the age of sixty-five is gonna need them."

He smiled back. "You're the best. At this point, I'm so hungry stale bread and warm water would be amazing."

"Your standards are just low enough, you might enjoy tonight's meatloaf and mashed potatoes. Enjoy your evening, sir." With another quick smile, she exited the room.

Everything smelled so good, his head swam with excitement. It had to have been well over twenty-four hours since he'd eaten since he'd slept through breakfast and lunch. As he shifted the table to his bed, his elbow knocked the nurse call button and television remote contraption on the floor. Groaning in annoyance, he pushed the tray away and got out of the bed, taking care to move slowly. The remote had slid under the bed a bit. He leaned down to grab it and his concussed head protested loudly. Little stars filled his vision, quickly replaced by spinning darkness.

Determined not to pass out and whack his head on the floor, he quickly shifted so that he could move from his knees to his backside. Once he'd managed to rest his bottom on the ice cold linoleum, he leaned against the bed and closed his eyes.

The dizziness took a lot longer to subside than he'd expected. The door opened again and footsteps sounded.

"Patrick?" Sylvia called out. He could hear the fear in that single word.

Lifting his uninjured arm to wave to her, he answered, "I'm over here."

The heels of her boots smacked against the floor as Sylvia closed the distance between them. In a few seconds she stood over him, looking down and shaking her head. "Are you okay?"

"I dropped the remote."

Sylvia chuckled as she leaned down to retrieve the contraption from under the bed. "Isn't that just like a man. Even a gunshot wound and a head injury can't come between a man and his remote control."

She set the remote on the bed, then offered a hand to Patrick. "Can you stand up if I help you or should I call a nurse?"

The nurse on duty had that take no prisoners attitude that might get him shackled to his bed if she knew what he'd done. He'd take his chances on his own. "The room has stopped tilting so I think I can get up myself."

"At least let me help you." She stepped over and tried to grab his hands but Patrick pulled away.

"I said I can do it myself."

Sylvia stepped back, her hands raised in mock surrender. "I guess losing your memory didn't affect your ego. Do it yourself then." She turned and walked away, not looking back at him.

When he heard her sit in the vinyl covered chair,

he realized what he'd done. Somehow, he had to get up off the slippery floor, using only one arm and not letting his dented brain make him dizzy.

"Damn it all," he murmured as he rolled to his good side.

Sylvia started to whistle. His blood almost literally boiled with his anger—at her, at the situation, and most of all because he had no damn idea who he was.

"Are you absolutely sure you don't want my assistance?" Sylvia asked, her foot tapping the floor.

"Fine. If it means that much to you, you can help me."

She got up and walked over to where he still sat. "Scoot forward. I'm going to get behind you and grab you under the arms."

He did as she said, trying to focus on the mission at hand and not any other reason why she might be grabbing him.

Sylvia sat on the edge of the bed and jammed her forearms under his arms. "On a count of three... one...two...three!"

She pulled on him as he used his good arm to brace himself and push up from the floor. His thighs burned with the effort but he finally got to his feet without passing out or ripping any stiches.

When he settled back on the bed, Patrick leaned against the pillows and let out a long exhale. He looked over at Sylvia, one eye closed and the other open. "Thanks."

She gave a nod. "No problem. Now, let me eat before my stomach digests itself."

Patrick picked up his fork and cut in to the meatloaf on his plate. "What's stopping you?"

Her response was the absolute last thing she expected from an agent of the United States government. Sylvia stuck her tongue out at him. With chewed up chicken all over it.

"So childish." He picked up his spoon and loaded it with one of the crispy green peas from his salad. Pulling the spoon back with one finger, he let go and flung the pea across the room. It hit Sylvia on the nose.

"*I'm* childish?" She picked the remains of the vegetable off her face. Scooping one of her own peas up, she threw it at Patrick smacking him in the center of the forehead.

"So, that's how you want to play this." He loaded the spoon once more with several of the peas and sent them airborne all at once. Sylvia laughed as she dodged the vegetable onslaught.

Before long, Sylvia was doubled over with laughter and the tiny green balls littered the floor. Her emerald eyes sparkled with mirth and mischief; a good look on her. Patrick raised his one good arm in surrender. "You win!"

"I'm a sharpshooter even with a spoon." She

pointed to Patrick's head. "There's some in your hair."

"What on earth is going on in here?" The door flew open and one of the nurses burst in, her hands on her hips. "This is a hospital! Full of sick people. We can hear you all the way down the hall."

"Sorry, ma'am." Patrick flashed her his best boy-next-door smile.

She walked over to the bed and started messing with the machines. "You disconnected something, it's beeping like crazy down at the desk."

He reached over and touched her arm. "Sorry, it won't happen again."

The older women blushed slightly and gave him a little smile. "I think it's about time you sent your friend home and got some rest. She can come back tomorrow."

Sylvia pulled out her badge and showed the nurse. "I'm a U.S. Marshal and this man is in protective custody."

She pressed a hand to her chest, her expression worried. "I had no idea. Are the patients here in danger?"

"The only one that needs to be worried is Patrick. Everyone else is perfectly safe. Once the doctor releases him in the morning, we will be out of your hair. But, until then, I stay put."

As Sylvia talked, the nurse moved toward the door. "Just try to keep it down in here then, please.

We have a lot of elderly patients on this floor and you were upsetting several of them."

"Yes, ma'am. Will do."

When she was gone, Patrick chuckled. "She made feel like we'd been caught having sex or something."

"Like that would ever happen." Sylvia shoveled a spoonful of mashed potatoes and gravy into her mouth. "Eww, they're cold."

They finished eating in silence. For some reason he refused to explore, Sylvia's comment had bruised his already sensitive ego. Maybe he didn't know his name or where he lived but he could see he had a pretty decent body, probably worked out and ate well. There was no reason any woman wouldn't be attracted to him.

Except that Sylvia had already proven she wasn't just any woman.

When he ate enough to take the edge off his hunger, Patrick pushed the tray table away. Reaching up, he clicked the switch that turned the light off over his bed. "I'm exhausted. I think I'll try to get some sleep now."

Sylvia nodded, a curious look in her eyes but she didn't say anything. Just ate her piece of chocolate cake and sipped her coffee.

CHAPTER FOUR

"Everything seems good. Let's get you signed out of here so your lady cop can try and figure out the mystery of where I should send my bill." Dr. Rivers laughed at his own joke. "I'd say I'm just kidding, but, I'm not." His toothy grin made Sylvia smile. The older man reminded her of her father. He probably had a special arsenal of Dad jokes just waiting to be deployed at a moment's notice.

"As soon as we crack the code, I'll let the hospital know everything," Patrick replied.

Dr. Rivers made a few notes in his computer then closed it up. "Funny thing is, I think you'll do exactly that. I'll send the nurse in with the discharge papers."

Sylvia pulled out her phone and sent a message to her boss. *Witness being released from hospital soon.*

Heading to the predetermined motel site to lay low and try to get his memory back.

She was half through her third level of *Candy Crush* when she got a reply. *Sending you a number for a contact at the FBI. Get one of the behavior people to do that hocus pocus hypnotizing stuff they do.*

Sylvia chuckled as she read the text. Her boss went way back; the "new-fangled" stuff, as he always called it, didn't impress him.

Getting desperate? she asked him.

Desperate times call for desperate measures. If I don't get you back here soon, your mother will be in my office raising hell.

He had a point there.

Okay. Send me the info. I'll call once we get settled in the safe room.

"Boyfriend?" Patrick asked, nodding toward her phone.

"Ugh, no. Boss." Sylvia tucked the phone in her bag and then stood up. Walking over to the sink, she ran her hands over her hair and splashed some cold water on her face. "First thing I'm gonna do is take a shower. I've got one change of clothes in my bag so I'm going to need to find a place to grab a couple things. For you, too."

He looked down at the hospital gown he wore. "What? You don't like my wardrobe?"

"While faded pink cotton might be all the rage

wherever you are from, it's awfully cold outside for something so light and airy."

"Fair enough. Think they will let me borrow it for a bit though? My other clothes are a little bloody."

Sylvia grabbed a plastic bag from under her chair and handed it to him. "While you were in the bathroom washing up, I went downstairs to the gift shop and found you a pair of sweats."

Patrick hugged the bag to his chest. "Be still my heart. Only two days together and she's already picking out my clothes."

"Why don't you go get changed so we can get out of here as soon as the paperwork is done?"

"Yeah, okay." Patrick went in the bathroom and closed the door.

Sylvia sat back down in her chair and stared at the bathroom door. Something about Patrick had been nagging at her. Something vaguely familiar, like they'd met somewhere at some other time. She just couldn't put her finger on it.

Her phone dinged the announcement of an incoming text. She pulled it from her bag and read the message containing the FBI contact. *He's expecting your call today.*

Got it, sir, she typed back.

The nurse that brought the discharge papers was much younger and more cheerful than the older, uptight woman assigned to him overnight. "Is our patient ready to get out of here?" she asked, walking past Sylvia and over to a tiny counter.

"Changing his clothes in the bathroom."

"I'm just about done!" Patrick called through the door.

"Are you his significant other?" the nurse asked her.

Sylvia showed the other woman her credentials. "No. Your patient is in protective custody until we figure out who he is and who tried to kill him."

The bathroom door opened and Patrick stepped out, clothed in the dark grey, terrycloth outfit and a big smile on his face. "It feels good to wear something that doesn't fly open every time I breathe. Although, it was tough to get this arm into the sleeve. Hurt like a mother—"

"You look like a prisoner on exercise break in the yard," Sylvia said. The nurse laughed but Patrick looked a little hurt.

"It's not like I have all the options you do."

Sylvia glared at him. "Options? I haven't changed my clothes since we met!"

The nurse giggled. "You two bicker like an old married couple."

"We do not!" Sylvia and Patrick said in unison.

Sylvia clapped a hand over her mouth. The nurse laughed and handed Patrick a stack of papers to read and sign. As she went over all the wound care instructions and such, Sylvia made a list on her phone's note app of all the things she needed to pick up at the store. When the last paper had been signed to set Patrick free, she grabbed her bag and headed out.

"Stay close, preferably a little bit behind me."

Talk about another hit to his fragile ego. "I'm not helpless."

She looked over her shoulder at him. "I understand that. But I have the gun and you are down one arm."

He nodded but didn't say anything as she led the way to the elevator. Once they were safely on their way to the first floor, Patrick spoke. "I feel a little like I'm in a *007* movie. I half expect to see James Bond drop from the ceiling."

Sylvia gave him her best eye roll. "Are you serious?"

Patrick shrugged his good shoulder. "I don't have much to go on but I suspect my life wasn't nearly this exciting."

The elevator slowed to a stop and the doors slid open. Sylvia stepped out first and surveyed the lobby. Satisfied that no one looked suspicious, she led the way toward the front doors. Mack had left her the rental car parked in the lot so she fished the keys out of her bag and hit the emergency button. The horn honked from about three hundred feet away.

Sylvia scanned the lot and saw nothing unusual. "Stay close once more."

"Yes, ma'am." Patrick stayed so close, she could feel the heat of his breath on her neck, causing tiny little ripples of goose flesh to form on her neck and shoulders.

They made it to the dark sedan that Mack had left her and got inside. She immediately hit the lock and turned the car on.

"Do you know where we are going yet?" Patrick asked.

Sylvia glanced over at him. "Just sit back, relax, and let it be a surprise."

Patrick sighed as he leaned back. "My whole life has become one big surprise."

The traffic stayed light all the way to the motel Sylvia had picked out. Old and run down on the outside, she knew the rooms had recently been redone and that each room opened on to an ocean view.

They'd stayed there once before about a year ago when she and Mack had done another witness transport. It had enough peeling paint and cracked concrete to make a good, safe layover spot.

"Here we are." Sylvia pulled the car into a parking spot beside a faded mural of a navy ship painting on the back of the building.

"Where?" Patrick glanced around. "An abandoned building?"

"The Sunset Motel." Sylvia opened the car door

and stepped out, grabbing her bag from the backseat. "Let's go. I don't like being so exposed."

"I hear the waves," Patrick commented as they followed the sidewalk around to the front of the building.

"This place sits right on the sand. All the rooms face the water. It's awesome." Sylvia pulled open the door and motioned to him to go in. "My partner and I have stayed here before on business. It's just nondescript enough to keep us off the radar."

"Welcome to the Sunset Motel. My name is Kassie. How may I help you this morning?" A grey-haired woman, wearing glasses that were at least two sizes too big for her petite size, greeted them with a warm smile.

"We'd like a room for the next couple of nights, please." Sylvia pulled out the identification of her alter-ego, Sarah Smart and showed it to the lady.

Kassie examined it then handed it back to her. "One bed or two?"

Sylvia took the i.d. and handed Kassie a credit card. "Two please. Something on the second floor would be great, if you have anything available."

"The sunsets over the water *are* beautiful this time of year." Kassie tapped a few things into the computer then pulled out two hotel keys. She handed them to Sylvia. "You're in luck. This is the off season so our best room is available. Enjoy your stay."

"Thank you, Kassie," Patrick said.

"Bless your heart, you do speak." Kassie pressed a hand to her chest.

Patrick looked, and sounded, confused. "What do you mean?"

"I just figured since your friend here—oh, you know what? Don't mind me. I'm just a crazy old woman with a good imagination. You two enjoy Virginia Beach now, ya hear?"

Sylvia bid the woman goodbye and left the office, Patrick close behind.

"What was that all about? Do I look like I'm a mute?"

"Calm down, Prince Patrick. She's just a bored old woman trying to entertain herself."

They climbed the steps to the second level and walked to the room they'd been assigned. When they reached the door, Sylvia went to insert the key but Patrick grabbed her wrist and turned her around, pressing her back to the door. He stepped in so close she could feel the rise and fall of his chest against hers. Her heart rate sped up, matching time with the thumping of her pulse in her ears as he put his hand on the door beside her head, essentially boxing her in against the door. He leaned down so that his lips were next to her ear and spoke, his voice deep and throaty.

"Please stop calling me Prince Patrick. I don't

know much, but I know I'm not royalty and I really don't like being mocked."

She could barely focus on the words his mouth formed as his stare pierced straight to her soul. Passing her tongue over her suddenly parched lips, Sylvia inhaled a shaky breath. "Would you please step back so I am not forced to shoot you?"

Or climb you like a tree and shove my tongue into your mouth.

Holy crap. Had she actually thought that about a witness in her custody?

He made no move to step back. The heat mixed with aggravation that rolled off of Patrick in waves had parts of her thawing that hadn't been warm in way too long. It took every single ounce of self-control she could muster not to wrap her arms around his neck and pull his lips to hers.

"I wasn't—mocking you. I'm sorry if you thought that." Even she could hear the shake in her voice.

Patrick lifted his head from by her ear and looked her in the eyes. "Believe me when I say, I don't want to be here anymore than you do. No matter how sexy your green eyes are, this is the last place I want to be. But, I have nowhere else to go and I would appreciate it if you would stop making a joke out of my situation."

He thought her eyes were sexy.

And he practically had her pinned to the steel door. Was he about to kiss her? She wanted him to kiss her. Nope. This couldn't happen. Sylvia sucked in a breath as she placed her palms against his chest and pushed against him. "Could you give me a little space please?"

Taking half a step back, Patrick remained close but at least she could almost breathe.

Fumbling with the key card, she reached behind her and slipped it into the lock after only three tries. The door opened into the room and Sylvia stumbled backward. Patrick tripped and fell against her, knocking them both to the floor. The heavy door slammed shut.

"Ouch." Patrick grunted as his injured shoulder made contact with her and then the floor.

"Are you okay?" Sylvia pressed a palm lightly to his cheek, the roughness of the two days' worth of stubble on his jaw scratching her skin.

Instead of answering her, Patrick rolled to the side, taking her with him so that she now lay on top of him.

Before she had time to think about it, Patrick crushed his lips to hers. Somewhere in the back of her mind a little voice screamed *No! He's your witness!*

A much louder voice told the little one to eat dirt.

Every hard inch of the complete stranger on top of her felt like it was designed to complement every inch of her body.

The room filled with music as the ring tone she'd assigned to her boss played. The musical interruption snapped her back to the present. She turned her head to the side, breaking off the kiss. "What are we doing?"

Patrick shook his head slowly. "I'm sorry. I shouldn't have—I mean, I have no idea what hit me. Kissing you is the last thing I want to do."

Sylvia sat upright, straddling his waist. "What the heck is that supposed to mean?"

Closing his eyes and exhaling, Patrick frowned. "I didn't mean that the way it sounded."

Sliding off of Patrick's hips, she leaned against the end of one of the beds. "There aren't too many ways to interpret it. Not that I care."

Liar.

Big, fat, dirty liar.

She cared. A lot. Way more than her terms of employment allowed for.

Patrick sat up and leaned against the other bed. "I don't know what came over me. I promise you I won't let it happen again."

Sylvia tucked her hair behind her ears and passed her tongue over her lips. "I need a shower. Desperately." Standing, she walked over and locked the door, slipping the latch closed so no one could get in without her hearing them break in. Grabbing her bag, she walked by Patrick, still sitting on the floor and entered the bathroom, locking the door behind her.

The tiny lavatory barely had space to undress

surrounded by the toilet, sink and tub. As she pulled her shirt over her head, Sylvia caught sight of herself in the mirror. Flushed and little wild eyed, she couldn't deny that the kiss had had an effect on her. As long as it didn't happen again, she'd just pretend this one hadn't happened either.

The steady hum of the water running in the shower tempted Patrick in ways he could never describe. Even though they'd been apart for several minutes, he still felt the softness of every curve of Sylvia's body where it had pressed against his. Something fell in the tub and his brain immediately imagined those curves draped in soaps suds and surrounded by the steam from the hot water.

"Get it together, man." He pulled himself up off the floor and sat on the bed, his back against the headboard. The wound in his shoulder throbbed as he waited for the dizziness in his head to subside. All the sudden movements had stirred his bruised brain up.

"I can't go on like this," he whispered into the empty room. "Why can't I remember anything?"

Sylvia's phone rang again. She'd never answered it before. Her boss would be worried. He thought about answering but the nausea won out. Patrick made no move to go to it. He just needed to sit for a bit then he could think about walking again.

The fall through the door had scrambled him up more than he wanted to admit. Pain medicine would make him sleepy though and he wanted to be awake for everything that might help him remember himself.

Sliding down the headboard he lay on his back. Every spring in the mattress seemed to press against his aching body. As he lay there, eyes closed, the water turned off in the bathroom. Sylvia's voice sounded through the door as she sang a song he didn't recognize. The off tune notes brought a smile to his lips.

Sylvia stepped out of the bathroom, wearing jeans and a maroon sweater. Using a towel, she worked at drying her wavy hair. She walked over to the bed and looked down at him. "You okay?"

"Aside from the fact that I am laying on a sheet of plywood filled with roofing nails, I'm as good as I can be."

"My FBI contact will be here in about thirty minutes to do the cognitive interview."

Patrick sat up, slowly, and leaned against the headboard again. "I don't get how another interview is going to make me remember who I am."

Sylvia sat on the edge of the other bed. "It's a little different. The agent has techniques to help you get into your own head."

"I don't want to be hypnotized."

Sylvia laughed. "This isn't a traveling road show. No one is dangling a watch in front of you and making you bark like a dog when a bell rings."

Patrick raised an eyebrow. "The oddest combination of a Bugs Bunny cartoon and Pavlov's dogs."

She shrugged. "I didn't have a lot of friends as a kid. Cartoons and books were my entertainment." Standing up, Sylvia walked back into the bathroom and returned with a hair brush.

"I find it hard to believe you weren't the home coming queen and student body president."

Sylvia sat back down and started working the brush through her tangled hair. "What would make you think that?"

He looked over at her, watching as she drew the brush through her hair. "You're incredibly self-confident. And you know you're gorgeous."

"I know no such thing." Sylvia focused her attention on her hair brush as a deep flush slowly climbed the fair skin of her neck and colored her cheeks. "My confidence is hard won. Carrying a gun helps too."

Patrick chuckled at her attempt to cover her embarrassment with a joke. The self-assured Marshal got embarrassed by a compliment.

A knock sounded at the door. Sylvia dropped the brush on the bed and reached for the gun she'd set on the nightstand when she'd come out of the bathroom. Holding a finger to her lips instructing him to be quiet, she crossed the carpet quietly. Holding her gun ready, she leaned forward and peered through the peep hole on the door.

Lowering her gun, Sylvia pulled the door open and motioned to the man outside to enter the room. He held his badge in his hand. Sylvia closed and bolted the door then extended her hand to the man that had just arrived. "It's nice to meet you, Agent Wright. Thank you for coming." She motioned toward Patrick. "This is our witness we hope you can help. He's quite frustrated."

"I can only imagine. Losing your memory is a loss of identity. Hopefully I can help you with some of that." Agent Wright pulled the one chair in the room up to the side of the bed, next to him. "You have to relax though. I need you to trust me."

Patrick nodded. "I'll do my best."

"Close your eyes and think back to the very first thing you remember," Agent Wright spoke softly, his voice calm.

"When I woke up in the alley with someone kicking me. Oh wait, I remember now. It was someone named Marshal Fairfax."

Sylvia coughed. "Yeah, sorry about that."

"You kicked an injured man?" Agent Wright asked.

"I thought he was dead. I didn't kick hard, just nudged him with the toe of my boot."

Agent Wright turned his attention back to

Patrick. "So, after Sylvia kicked you, what else do you remember? A certain sound, or a smell maybe?"

"I could definitely smell the garbage in the dumpster. And something else. Like smoke from a cigar mixed with rotting meat."

He could hear Agent Wright tapping notes in to his phone before he asked his next question. "How did the ground feel?'

Patrick shrugged. "Hard? Cold? How does ground usually feel."

"Okay." Agent Wright jotted a few more notes into his phone. "Do you remember how you got there? On the ground, I mean."

Patrick traveled back to the night in his mind. "I remember standing there."

"Good!" Agent Wright patted his arm. "What could it be that had led you to that place?"

Patrick went back to that cold, dark alley and the noise that had drawn him into it in his head. "I heard a noise. Someone—shouting? Crying, maybe? Yeah, crying. I definitely heard someone sobbing."

"Was it a woman?"

Patrick squeezed his eyes tight and willed his brain to remember something. "I'm not sure but I think it was a man. And I definitely heard a man's voice."

"That would be the killer and our other witness who is now dead," Sylvia said.

"That's very good. Do you remember hearing or seeing anything else?" Agent Wright asked.

Just like someone had turned off the television, Patrick's mind went blank and he opened his eyes. "That's it. The rest is like when we were kids and we tried to catch sight of a boob on the porn channels that were staticky."

Agent Wright laughed. "A true rite of passage for every teen boy in the eighties. Today's kids don't understand the trials we endured."

Sylvia let out an exaggerated sigh. "Men. Just like boys only taller and balder."

Agent Wright pretended to be offended as he ran his fingers through his thick salt and pepper hair. "I've got a full head of gorgeous hair."

"Can we try again?" Sylvia asked. "Maybe try to figure out Patrick's identity?"

Agent Wright shook his head. "I can come back tomorrow but I think we've done enough for today."

Patrick sat up. "I want to go again."

"You've got a head injury. I don't want to push your brain too hard."

He swung his legs over the side of the bed and stood up. "I'll be in the bathroom."

"Patrick." Sylvia touched his arm as he passed and but he shrugged it off and kept on walking.

"Let him go," he heard Agent Wright say. "He's got a lot to process."

Patrick stepped into the bathroom and closed the

door. Leaning on the sink, he stared at his reflection. "Why can't you remember your own damned name?"

The tears he'd tried to hold back fell freely, making him even madder at himself.

Through the door he could hear the others talking; too softly to make out the words they said. Eventually the motel room door opened and closed.

Using his good hand, he splashed some cold water on his face and dried it with a towel. A quiet knock on the door caught his attention, followed by Sylvia's voice. "Patrick? Agent Wright is gone, if you want to come out now."

"Leave me alone, please."

"I want to help."

He grabbed the door knob and flung the door open. "You want to *help*? You know what I think? You want to find your killer. That's what you want."

Sylvia held her ground. "Of course, I do! It's my job to find him but it's also to protect you! And part of protecting you is helping you figure out who you are before the man that wants you dead does!"

If someone asked him years later, he'd never be able to explain what he did next. Sylvia's untamed hair, half dry and half wet hanging loose around her shoulders and framing those passion filled emerald eyes became all he could focus on. He stepped forward, she stepped back, out of his reach. They played that cat and mouse game all the way across the room until her back was against the dented steel door to the room. Sylvia never broke eye contact and with each step her passion for her job became replaced with something new. Desire? He told himself that's what it was, right before he crushed his mouth to hers for the second time that day. This time, she'd never be able to deny she'd wanted that kiss too. Sylvia melted against him, their bodies perfectly matched. All the anger, frustration and a million other emotions he couldn't name consumed that kiss. Consumed him.

Sylvia wrapped her arms around his neck, pulling him in closer. Pain shot through his injured arm but he ignored it for the onslaught of fire building in his veins as he let his body take over for his common sense.

Suddenly, Sylvia's arms were no longer wrapped around him. Instead they pushed at his chest as she turned away. The kiss ended as abruptly as it had begun.

"It happened again." He touched her cheek lightly. "It was pretty amazing."

She held up a hand. "It was—really good. But it really can't keep happening. We're both stressed and high-strung right now. With that much passion, something was bound to happen." She grabbed a key card off the table. "I'm going to hit the vending machine for some snacks and a water. You want anything?"

He shook his head. "Nah. I don't have much of an appetite at the moment."

"I'll be right back."

Sylvia walked out, letting the door slam shut behind her. Patrick picked up a pillow off the bed and threw it across the room, landing it in the trash can in the corner. "Nice work, idiot. You just pissed off the one person on this planet that actually knows you exist."

CHAPTER FIVE

Even with the sun shining, the air felt brisk. Sylvia jogged down to the main lobby where she'd seen some vending machines. They definitely needed to order some real food for dinner but she could get by on snacks for the moment.

Dropping some coins in the machine, she chose some chips, a chocolate bar and a drink and then headed back to the room.

Sliding the key in to the reader, she pushed the door open. "Hey, Patrick, we should really think about having a pizza delivered or something."

Both beds were empty. The door to the bathroom stood closed so she walked over there and spoke again. "You hear me in there? I'm starving and these chips aren't going to even take the edge off. What do you want on a pizza? The agency is treating."

No reply.

In fact, the entire room felt eerily quiet. Reaching out, she turned the knob slightly. Not locked. She shoved it open. "Patrick? You in there?"

Of course, she could see immediately that the tiny room stood empty. Panic moved in quick. How could she have lost a *second* witness in less than a week. Turning around slowly, she searched the room for signs of a struggle. Nothing looked out of place.

"Where did you go?" Sylvia asked the empty room.

Grabbing her key card again, she bolted from the room. Patrick couldn't have gotten far. She'd only been gone a couple of minutes. Unless someone had taken him. And had a really fast car. Then he could be anywhere.

Praying that wasn't what happened, she first searched all around the motel with no success.

"Okay, if I were a confused man with no memory of who I was, where would I go?"

The sound of waves crashing against the shore caught her attention. Taking off at a sprint, she ran the length of the path set up between the motel property and the sand. When she made it to the end, she stopped running and looked around. The wind whipped grains of sand against her face making it nearly impossible to see anything.

"Patrick!" The wind carried her voice away.

Walking with her head down, Sylvia followed the dunes toward the fishing pier. "Patrick? Are you out here?"

Still nothing. The waves crashed steadily against the sand, worrying her that maybe Patrick had done something stupid. As she stumbled under the pier and used a wood piling to block the wind, she saw what she'd been looking for. Patrick, sitting on the sand, his back against one of the wood pilings. He cradled his injured arm against his chest, his head leaned back and eyes closed.

Sylvia trudged through the sand and dropped down beside him. "What are you doing out here?"

Patrick shrugged. "I needed some air."

She leaned over and bumped him lightly with her shoulder. "Usually, when one is in protective custody, they don't disappear like this. You really scared me."

"Sorry about that," he said the words but they were empty.

"Yeah, well, I'd appreciate it if you didn't do it again."

He rolled his head to the side and opened one eye to look at her. "Why do you even care?"

"You're my witness and—"

He slapped a hand to his thigh. "I can't even *remember*! And let's not forget about the way I practically attacked you. *Twice*."

Sylvia reached over and threaded her fingers with

his. Squeezing his hand lightly, she tugged him closer to her so she could rest her head on his shoulder. "We were both completely willing participants in that kiss."

"We were?" He turned to look down at her.

"Absolutely. I only stopped it because of my job. And, because we have no idea if you are married, engaged, or whatever. I can't be the other woman. Been there, done that, and have the t-shirt. I will *never* do it again."

The wind kicked up an icy gust that made her shiver. Patrick let go of his hand and wrapped his arm around her, pulling her in close. "I'm sorry I scared you. I'm just so confused and overwhelmed. I thought that FBI guy would fix me."

"It's a process. You remembered more than you did before the interview. Maybe tomorrow will bring it all back. The doctor said it would be quick and unexpected."

Patrick laughed, with no humor. "I don't know for sure, but I'm pretty sure I am not a patient person."

"How about we head back to the motel, order some dinner, and watch stupid television for a while."

He squeezed her shoulders lightly in a hug. "I have a better idea."

"Oh?"

Patrick pulled away from her and got to his feet.

"Let's go back to the alley where the guy shot me and see if that triggers anything."

Sylvia stood up as well, brushing sand from her jeans. She hugged herself against another gust of wind. "I'm not so sure that's such a good idea." Sylvia started walking back toward the motel.

Patrick followed her. "Why not?"

"What if someone else recognizes you?"

He frowned. "Wouldn't that be a good thing?"

Sylvia shook her head. "Depends on who it is." She rubbed her hands up and down her arms trying to keep warm. The look on Patrick's face nearly crushed her heart. "You know what? If you want to go, I'll take you. Maybe it *will* help. I just need to grab my coat from the room."

"Thank you, Marshal Fairfax."

She laughed. "I'm pretty sure we've gotten past the formalities. Just call me Sylvia."

Patrick laughed too and reached for her hand. "Okay, Sylvia."

Knowing full well she shouldn't encourage any more contact with him, Sylvia ignored the little voice of her conscience and moved in close to him. She told herself it was for warmth but she definitely didn't believe herself.

Ten minutes later, they were driving down Atlantic Avenue. Sylvia pulled into a parking space about two blocks from where they'd found Patrick and they walked the rest of the way.

"So, this is it?" Patrick stood next to her at the end of the alley where he'd been left for dead.

Sylvia pulled one hand out of a pocket and pointed to the green dumpster about halfway down the narrow space. "You were right there, on the ground by that trash can."

"And the other guy?" Patrick asked.

"All the way at the end." She motioned to a dark corner of the alley. "According to the investigation, no one heard a thing."

Patrick walked over to the dumpster and looked down. There was a dark spot on the pavement. "Is that my blood?"

Sylvia joined him by the stain. "Yeah. I'm sorry you had to see that."

"I'm not." He turned and faced the building opposite of where they stood. "This is the bit I remembered today. Standing here, hearing the other man begging for his life, a gun pointed at me." Patrick closed his eyes. "That's it though. That's where it ends."

"Nothing's coming back to you about how you ended up here?"

Patrick shook his head. "Not a thing."

She could hear the frustration in his voice. Not knowing who you are or where you're from had to be a heavy load to carry.

She rubbed a hand on his back. "Let's head back to the motel now."

"Yeah, okay."

Patrick stayed quiet during the ride back. When they got inside the room, he headed straight to the bathroom. Sylvia grabbed a shirt to sleep in out of her bag and headed in to the bathroom when Patrick was done. By the time she got out, he was in bed and sound asleep. Sylvia took the chair and jammed it under the doorknob, then placed her gun on the table next to her bed.

Crawling into bed, she turned off the bedside light and opened her favorite word game on her phone. At some point she fell asleep, the phone hitting her on the nose as she dropped it and waking her enough to set it on the table next to her gun before she fell back asleep again.

* * *

"Please! You don't have to do this! I won't say anything to anyone. I promise!"

The man with the gun stepped in close. Close enough that Patrick could see down the barrel of the gun.

"No!" He sat up, his heart racing and sweat pouring down his face and neck. The darkness felt the same but the sounds and smells were different.

"Patrick? Are you okay?" A sleepy, familiar voice called out to him. And then he realized where he was and that the whole thing had just been a dream.

"I'm sorry I woke you, Sylvia. I had a bit of a bad dream."

She got out of bed and came over to sit beside him. He could smell the floral scent of her shampoo and it had an interesting calming effect on him. She wrapped an arm around his shoulders. "Were you dreaming about it?"

"I guess." Just having her close had already begun to calm his racing pulse. "I'm sorry I woke you. It won't happen again."

She smiled. "Don't go making promises you can't keep. I don't mind if you do wake me up again. I've had my fair share of memories haunt me in the dark of night. It's those wee hours of the morning that can be the worst."

"I bet you've seen some stuff." He'd not really thought about the job that she did. Sylvia had a bird's eye view to some of the worst the world had to offer.

"It was worse when I was a cop. When the lights go out and the moon shows up, so do all the crazies."

"You were a cop?" This shouldn't have surprised him but it did.

She fiddled with the hem of the sheet. "Durham, North Carolina. Almost ten years."

"What made you leave?"

Sylvia seemed to retreat into her own head as soon as the question came out of his mouth. They sat in silence for a long time before she finally took a deep breath and spoke. "I went undercover a lot. Deep cover. The kind where it's easy to forget who you really are. Living the lie day in and day out messes with your mind. My last undercover job went bad. Like, really bad. I nearly didn't make it out. That's when I decided I was done. I still loved law enforcement but I couldn't stay there. I'd forever be that girl and I needed to move on."

She closed her eyes and took a few deep breaths.

"Did someone hurt you?" he asked, already angry at the person who could do such a thing.

"I got caught up in a human trafficking scheme. Someone put me up for auction and I was sold to a foreign national looking for a sex slave. Literally. Thank the Lord my people got me out of there. But they were almost too late. He took me on a boat and had almost crossed into international waters."

He turned on the bed so that they faced each other. "Oh, Sylvia. He didn't—hurt you—did he?"

"Let's just say he came too close for comfort. I still dream about it. Doesn't help that some of the guys at the department found it humorous I'd been sold on the black market. They had no idea how close I'd come—" That distant look returned to her eyes. Patrick sat quietly, waiting for her to work through her demons. He certainly understood what that felt like.

Patrick reached for her hand. "I'm so sorry that

happened to you. I wish I could take the memories away."

She laughed. "The whole experience is part of me. It has shaped me as a person and a law enforcement officer. I'm not saying I'm glad it happened but I have accepted it. And you will learn to do the same. Eventually. It's hard being faced with your own mortality."

"I think we are both a hot mess." He leaned back on his pillow and patted the bed next to him. "You can stay here if you want to. Maybe we will both sleep better."

Even when she frowned at him, Sylvia still looked beautiful. "What if—I mean, I'm really concerned you might be married or something."

"I was thinking about that." He held out his hand. "Look. No ring tan."

"No what?" Sylvia sounded confused.

"No ring tan. If I'd been wearing a wedding band, there would be a tan line or an impression or something. But, there isn't. Plus, I just don't *feel* like there is someone in my life, if that makes any kind of sense at all."

"It makes perfect sense, even if it shouldn't. I still have my job to worry about though."

He held up his good hand. "I've only got one functioning arm and the other one hurts like a son of a bitch. I promise, I'm just going to sleep."

The thought of her next to him all night had a calming effect he couldn't put into words. He strongly suspected that even before the accident he hadn't slept next to another person for a very long time.

She looked conflicted. Finally, though, she smiled and nodded. "I like the way you think."

Sylvia fluffed a pillow then stretch out on the bed beside him. They lay that way for a long time, facing each other before she spoke. "I'm probably breaking a hundred different policies right now."

A couple of random waves fell across Sylvia's forehead. He reached up and pushed the silky hair back behind her ear, marveling at the softness of her skin. "I promise not to tell." The blush that colored her cheeks made her practically glow in the moonlight that passed through the break in the drapes. "We aren't doing anything to talk about anyway. Just sleeping."

She raised an eyebrow. "Not much sleeping happening at the moment."

"I'm afraid I will never remember who I am."

Sylvia shifted gears quickly at his sudden change of topic. "You heard the doctors. It's temporary. All you need is one thing to jog your memory."

"What if that one thing never happens?"

The feel of her touch as Sylvia reached over and pressed her palm lightly to his cheek kicked his pulse rate up several notches. He wrapped his fingers around her wrist and held it there for a few long moments, enjoying the closeness as much as the sensations it caused within him. "Well, I've got your back until it does."

"I appreciate that. You know, if my back survives this mattress."

Sylvia laughed. "What is it with you and mattresses? You have complained about every bed you've been in, including the ambulance stretcher."

Patrick shrugged. "I have no idea. Did I really complain about the stretcher?"

"Yeah. And the gurney in the E.R."

He lifted his head to look at her. "Seriously?"

"Seriously."

"Maybe it's the head injury." He lay back down against the pillow. "The constant ache is annoying. I have to focus on something else."

Sylvia pressed her fingertips lightly to his forehead. "I'm sorry it's still hurts." She began a gentle massage to one of his temples before trailing her fingers lightly across his forehead and rubbing the other one."

Patrick stifled a moan and pulled the blanket over him to hide the obvious effects of her touch. "That feels amazing. It almost makes the hurt go away."

"I was pretty angry about being stuck babysitting you."

He frowned. "Gee, thanks."

"Not you personally, just being stuck here. Not going home. Not that I have all that much to go home to. I mean, Larry might be dead when I get back, but that's not a huge deal."

"Someone could die and it's not a big deal?" Patrick couldn't believe she'd been so nonchalant about a death.

Sylvia smiled, pressing a fingertip to his lips. "Larry is a goldfish."

"Ah! Okay. You had me worried for a minute. Wondered if I should stay awake all night."

She winked at him. "I've never been known to sleep shoot anyone but I suppose there is a first for everything."

He pulled the covers the rest of the way across the bed so that they covered Sylvia too. "'ll wrap you in this burrito of polyester and you won't be able to."

She pulled the blankets up to her chest. "I suppose we ought to get some sleep. Who knows what excitement tomorrow will bring."

"With any luck, I'll wake up in the morning and remember everything. My name, who the killer was, and how the heck I ended up with a name tag calling me Prince Patrick."

"I don't know, it's kind of fun being able to say I'm sleeping with a man of royalty."

Patrick chuckled. "It suits you, m'lady."

"Good night, Prince Patrick of the Sunset Motel."

"Good night, U.S. Marshal Sylvia Fairfax."

He watched as Sylvia's eyelids slowly closed, marveling at the way her long lashes fanned across her cheeks. Her breathing settled in a regular pattern as Sylvia slipped off in to her dreams. Patrick lay there a very long time watching the peace that sleep brought to Sylvia and envying her ability to relax so completely. Every inch of his body had been tense since the moment he woke up in that alley.

CHAPTER SIX

Patrick had been right. The mattress left an awful lot to be desired but she felt warm and cozy and comfortable snuggled under the blankets. As she lay there, contemplating how badly she needed the facilities, a loud banging sounded on the motel room door.

Sylvia jumped out of bed, grabbing her gun from the nightstand.

"What's going on?" Patrick sat up, rubbing his eyes.

"Shhh...We've got company," Sylvia whispered, moving quietly to the door.

Someone pounded again. "Fairfax! Open the damn door!"

"Mack?" she yelled through the door. "That you?"

"No! it's the damned tooth fairy. Of course, it's me! Who else would it be?"

Sylvia pulled the door open and motioned her partner inside. "What are you doing here? I thought you'd be at the Waffle House near Research Triangle by now."

"I was. I came back. Boss thought you might need some back up." He looked from her mostly unused bed to the one Patrick still lay in. "I can see you don't need me at all."

Sylvia lowered her gun and punched Mack on the arm. "You don't *see* anything. Nothing to see. Now, why are you really here?"

He shrugged. "I had to make a delivery in New York and the boss asked me to see if you needed anything on my way home. I have less than a week until retirement and the agency is determined to work me to death."

"Do I know you?" Patrick asked from the bed. "You seem familiar."

Mack looked over at the other man and raised an eyebrow. "I was there in the alley when they found you. How's the brain?"

"Mack—" Sylvia's voice held a note of warning.

"It's fine." Patrick pushed back the covers and stood up. "I'm going to get a shower."

Sylvia watched as he walked in to the bathroom and closed the door.

"He needs some clean clothes. All he has is the outfit I grabbed at the hospital."

"I figured as much." Mack held up a duffle bag. "I

had my wife grab a few things for both of you and pack them in here. You're about the same size as Susan. I didn't know about him, so I grabbed some track pants and long sleeve shirts from my closet."

"You're the best. Thanks, Mack."

Her partner set the bag on the little table. "I know. How about I go hustle up some breakfast while you two get showered and dressed. The FBI guy wants to talk to the witness again, in his office this time. See if he can help him remember more details about that night."

"How do you know that and I don't?" Sylvia asked.

"Check your messages. I bet you got a text."

Sylvia grabbed her phone and sure enough, she had a message from Agent Wright asking her to come to the office with Patrick.

"Did he text you too?" Sylvia held her phone up for Mack to see.

Mack nodded, fiddling with his keys in the pocket of his coat. "Um, yeah. I talked to him earlier. I'm going to get that food now."

"Okay, thanks. And really thank you for the clean clothes."

He stopped, his hand on the door knob. "Just doing my job. After I feed you two, I'm heading back to Raleigh. Is there anything else you need while I'm out?"

Sylvia shook her head. "I don't think so."

Mack gave a little salute. "Okay then, be back in a jiffy."

Every now and then Mack showed the generational gap between them, reminding of her own father, who had been about the same age as Mack when he died.

The door closed. Sylvia opened the duffle and found two sets of clothes for each of them. Mack had been right; his wife wore her exact size in jeans and tops. Laying out her clothes on her bed and Patrick's on his, she went over and knocked on the bathroom door.

The water in the shower turned off. "Be out in a minute," Patrick called from inside.

"Mack's wife sent you some clothes. Nothing fancy but they are clean. I put them on your bed."

The door opened. Patrick stood in front of her, towel slung low on his hips. Little droplets of water glistened on the hard planes of his chest and wet waves fell over his forehead. Sylvia fought back the desire to push those damp locks away from his face. Her hand twitched as she gave herself a mental talking to.

The water proof bandage on his shoulder reminded her of why they were there and dialed her thoughts back in to where they should be.

Patrick smiled. The kind of smile that could bring a weaker woman to her knees. "Please tell Mrs. Mack

I said thank you. I had no interest in putting my other clothes back on."

Sylvia laughed. "Her name is Susan McCoy. I'll be sure to pass the message on to her."

"Thank you." An incredibly sexy flush filled in over his features, making her want to kiss him on every place that had turned that beautiful blush.

She shook her head to clear the images and motioned to the bathroom. "If you're done, I'll shower too."

Patrick smiled and stepped into the room. "Of course."

"Thank you." Before closing the door, Sylvia stuck her head back out. "Mack went out to find us some food. He will be back soon."

"Excellent. I'm starved." He pressed his hand to his abdomen, bringing her gaze where she knew it shouldn't be.

Without saying anything, Sylvia stepped into the bathroom and closed the door, collapsing against it and taking several deep breaths.

Since she'd left the police department, she hadn't had any interest in a single man. The whole incident there had left a horrible taste in her mouth concerning romance. "So, why now?" she whispered. "Why this man? He has no idea who is or what has happened to him."

Stepping over to the shower, she turned the water on and undressed. As she stepped in to the hot spray, she closed her eyes, focusing only on the water pelting her skin. A clear head is what she needed. Sleeping in the same bed with Patrick after confessing what had happened to her had blurred the lines of professionalism. She really just needed to refocus and get her head back in the game.

It felt so much harder than it ought to be.

Once Sylvia closed the bathroom door, Patrick let his towel drop to the floor. The clothes Susan McCoy sent didn't include underwear. He'd just have to make do. The clean shirt and pants felt so good, he didn't even care that he had to go all natural underneath. He pulled on the pants first, then grabbed the towel and used it to dry his hair and upper body a bit better.

The full-length mirror on the back of the closet door told a story that he didn't like. His shoulder still ached but at least pain no longer sliced straight through him like the bullet had. The bandages needed changing. Patrick walked over to the corner where he'd stowed the hospital bag and grabbed the supplies the nurse had sent with him. Laying everything out on the table, he sat down and pulled first the front bandage off, then the back one. Using the closet mirror, he could see the angry redness of the exit wound. It had been larger and more tore up than the entrance wound. With a small gauze pad, he smeared some of the anti-bacterial ointment on the front wound then opened one of the self-stick square bandages the nurse had told him to use and pressed it over the injury.

The back would be a bit tougher. Reaching over his shoulder, and using the mirror for assistance, he smeared the ointment on his back. Opening the self-stick bandage next, he tried to figure the best way to do that himself.

"It always looks so easy on television." Picking up the bandage, Patrick moved over to where the mirror hung and turned sideways. Using the reflection as his guide, he stretched his good arm as much as he could to reach over his shoulder and get the bandage in the right place. It ended up being easier than he thought.

"Nice work, if I do say so myself." As he picked up his shirt and stuck his arms in the holes, someone knocked on the door. Patrick dropped the shirt on the bed, walked over and peered through the tiny peep hole.

"Come on, man. Let me in. It's Sylvia's partner, Mack."

Water still ran in the bathroom, meaning Sylvia was still showering. He hated to disturb her over this so he didn't try to call to her, instead he positioned himself behind the door and turned the knob. As soon as he opened the door, Mack shoved his way in to the room. Patrick pushed the door closed.

Patrick glared at Mack. There was something about the other man he just didn't like. "What the heck? You in some kinda hurry?"

Mack set a couple of bags on one of the beds. "You left me standing out there, exposed. I coulda been shot."

"No one knows we're here."

"You can never be sure of that." Mack walked over to the bathroom and rapped on the door. "Let's go, Fairfax! Grub's here!"

"Be out in a minute!" Sylvia called as the water turned off.

Mack looked over at him, his forehead creased deep with disapproval. "You gonna put a damn shirt on or what?"

"Does my bandage offend you?" Patrick asked, eyes narrowed as he watched Mack pull food out of the bags.

"I've seen plenty of gunshot wounds *without* bandages. But I'm a southern boy and my Mama never let anyone sit at her table without all their clothes on."

Patrick grabbed his shirt off the bed and pulled it on, stifling a groan when he had to lift his arm to slip it into a sleeve.

"Still hurtin', huh?" Mack didn't sound the least bit concerned for Patrick's pain.

"I'm fine."

The bathroom door opened and Sylvia stepped into the room. "Something smells so good. What'd you get, Mack?"

"Flapjacks, sausage gravy with biscuits, eggs, waffles, bacon and sausage." Mack motioned to the several Styrofoam containers he placed on the bed.

"You feeding an army?" Sylvia opened the first container and moaned. "Belgian waffles are my favorite."

"I know." He tossed Sylvia a plastic fork and knife then turned to Patrick. "The sausage gravy is mine. You can have what you want from what's left."

Patrick picked up a tray of eggs, bacon and toast. "This is great, thanks."

Mack took a big forkful of his biscuit and gravy. "Had to feed my girl."

He winked at Sylvia who waved her fork at him. "Thanks, partner."

Sylvia's phone played a little tune indicating a text message had just come in. She set her food down and picked it up off the nightstand. Patrick watched as she read the message.

"What's up, Fairfax? You look worried?" Mack nodded in her direction.

She put the phone in the pocket of her jeans. "I have to take Patrick to the FBI field office in a little bit for a second interview."

"You already knew that," Patrick said.

"I know." Sylvia took another bite of waffle. "Something just doesn't feel right though, and I don't know why."

Mack shoveled some more food into his mouth. "It'll be fine," Mack said, around a mouthful of biscuit.

Sylvia nodded. "Yeah, I know. I guess I'm just anxious to settle this case."

They finished eating in silence. Patrick watched both Sylvia, who was lost in her own thoughts and Mack, who still didn't sit right with him. He ate the last of his eggs and tossed the foam box back in the bag it had come from.

"Well, I think it's time for me to head on back to Raleigh." Mack pulled a handkerchief from his jacket pocket and dabbed the corner of his lips.

Sylvia looked up from slipping her boots on. "You just got here this morning."

"It was just a mission of mercy, Fairfax. Susan insisted I bring you some clothes."

"You drove over four hours to bring clothes?" Patrick asked.

Mack held his hands in the air. "What can I say? I'm a good guy."

"Of course, you are. The best partner too. The agency won't be the same without you." Sylvia motioned to her outfit. "Thank Susan for the clothes please."

"Will do." Mack gave her a little salute then

turned to Patrick. "Good luck with the head shrinker." With a wave, he opened the door and left.

"How long have you worked with him?" Patrick asked Sylvia.

She shrugged sitting on one of the beds and pulling out her phone from her pocket. "Since I joined the Marshals."

"Do you trust him?"

Sylvia looked up from the message she was reading on her phone. "With my life. Why?"

Patrick walked over and sat beside her on the bed. "Something just keeps nagging at me and I can't figure out what it is."

"About Mack?"

"I don't know." He picked up her hand and laced his fingers through hers. "Every time he is around, I feel like there is a memory or a thought just out of reach. Something I should know or remember. Maybe it's because he was there when I first came to in the alley."

Sylvia leaned her head onto his shoulder. "Hope-fully today you will regain enough of your memory that we can start to piece together who you are." She held up her phone. "The text I just got? I asked someone back in the office to run the name Patrick through all the missing person's data bases. Nothing came back that could have even remotely been you."

"So, no one is missing me? Is that what that means?"

Sylvia looked up at him and frowned. "I don't know. Maybe your family just doesn't realize you are missing yet? You could have been here on vacation."

"Or maybe I don't have a family?"

She reached up and pressed a palm gently to his cheek. "I highly doubt that. We do need to get going. Agent Wright is expecting us at the Norfolk office in thirty minutes."

"Okay." Patrick let go of her hand and stood up.

Sylvia rose to her feet as well. "Bring your things with you. If this goes well, we won't have to come back here. You can use that bag Mack brought."

Five minutes later, they walked out of the hotel room. He followed Sylvia to the car, the ocean air crisp and the wind gusts chilling him straight through to the bone.

He rubbed his hands up and down his arms for warmth, grimacing at the ache in his injured shoulder. "I really think it should be warmer here. I mean, Virginia Beach. It's a beach town and a vacation destination, right?"

Sylvia laughed as she opened the trunk and dropped her bag inside. Patrick followed suit. "The weather here has confused me every time I've been here." She motioned to the car. "Get in, before you freeze."

As they pulled onto the interstate, Sylvia looked up into the review mirror and frowned.

"What's wrong?" he asked, looking behind them.

"There's a black sedan, about three back, that seems to be following us. Every time I change lanes, they do too."

Patrick turned and looked back again. "Maybe it's a coincidence."

"Maybe. But I don't think so. Hold on, I'm going to try and lose them." Sylvia hit the gas pedal hard. The sudden burst of speed pushed him hard against the seat. Searing pain shot through his chest but he ignored it.

As Sylvia drove faster, the black car sped up too. He watched as she expertly maneuvered them in and out of traffic before slipping off the interstate at the next exit. Without slowing down, she sped off the exit ramp and straight into a nearby neighborhood. Two quick turns later and Patrick let go of the breath he'd been holding.

"I think we're good," Sylvia finally said.

As soon as the words left her mouth, the back window of the car shattered.

"Did someone just try to shoot at us?" he asked.

CHAPTER SEVEN

"Someone *did* shoot at us."

Two more shots slammed into the car.

"Get down!" Sylvia shouted as she floored the gas pedal. The sedan jerked forward as Patrick ducked down. "Stay out of sight. It's you they want to get."

"Don't worry about me! Just get us out of here!"

At the next corner, she whipped the wheel and turned the car to the right. One more block down, she turned left. The momentum lifted the passenger side tires off the road briefly but Sylvia kept going. She knew from a previous visit to Virginia Beach they weren't far from a police precinct.

"Are they still following us?" Patrick asked from the floor boards. Before she could answer, another shot slammed in to the car, striking and shattering the back seat window on the driver's side.

"Stay down there! I'll have us to a safe place in a minute."

When she reached the next stop light, she made a quick right and pulled in to the parking lot of the police station. Pulling in between two patrol cars, she kept an eye on the black sedan as it rolled slowly past the precinct. The tint on the windows prevented her from seeing inside.

When their pursuer reached the next intersection, they turned left and disappeared in the traffic.

"You can get up now," she said.

Patrick unfolded himself off the floor of the car and leaned back in the passenger seat. She could see his hands shaking from the adrenaline dump.

"You okay?" she asked.

"I'm fine. At least, I will be when my heart stops trying to jump out of my chest." He looked over at her. "How are you so calm?"

Sylvia laughed. "Just another day at the office."

"You get shot at a lot?"

"Not really, no. But the adrenaline rush is nothing new to me. That's why you feel the way you do. It will clear up soon."

Sylvia pulled her phone from her pocket. "I don't think we're going to make our appointment on time. Let me tell Agent Wright we will be late and then we will get back on the interstate and tried to figure out who wants you dead. Again."

She typed out the message and sent it. Then,

with one last look around, she backed out of the spot and headed to the road. Five minutes later they were back on the interstate, headed to Norfolk. With the two broken windows, the wind was brutal. Patrick turned the heat on high and aimed all the vents at himself.

Patrick hugged himself, teeth chattering. "I can't believe this weather. It's only November. Right? It's November, isn't it? I hate not knowing things!"

In that moment, Sylvia's heart broke a little for Patrick. Not forgetting the fact that he was technically in protective custody and it was her job to find out what he knows, she couldn't help but feel bad for him. Not knowing who you are or where you came from felt like one of Dante's levels of hell to her, a person who planned every single detail of her life. This unexpected little custody job of hers had thrown her through enough of a loop. She couldn't imagine how he must feel.

"It is November. Thanksgiving is in about ten days."

"Wonderful. Where are you spending Thanksgiving, Patrick? Gee, I don't know. Because I don't know where I live!"

She reached over and patted his arm. "I promise we will figure it out."

Patrick reached up and lightly squeezed her hand. "Maybe."

Sylvia steered the now limping car onto the off

ramp. A couple minutes later she pulled in to the parking lot of the FBI field office. As she turned the vehicle off, it shuddered a little. One of the bullets must have done more damage than she thought.

"Let's get inside and talk to Agent Wright. I need to find us a different motel to stay at while you are with him."

"Why?" Patrick stepped from the car and braced himself with both hands.

Sylvia gave him a long look. "Are your knees and legs feeling weak?"

"I'm fine. Just still a little dizzy when I first stand up from the concussion."

She nodded. That made sense. "Let's get you inside. I don't like being so exposed."

Sylvia led Patrick to the main entrance. She held up her ID at the camera and the door buzzed open.

Agent Wright greeted them in the small lobby. "Marshal Fairfax, it's good to see you again. How's our witness today?"

"Still don't know who I am, if that's what you're asking?" Patrick replied.

Agent Wright chuckled. "Yes, that's what I'm asking. You both look a bit frazzled. I hope you found our office easily?"

"Finding it wasn't the issue. Getting here in one piece as someone fired on us was the issue."

"Someone shot at you?" Agent Wright stopped

walking and looked them both up and down. "Either of you hurt?"

"No. No. We're both fine." Sylvia waved a hand of dismissal. "It just means we need another place to stay when we leave here. Our location has probably been compromised."

"I'll have our office manager get you some numbers. Maybe staying here in Norfolk would be less conspicuous."

Sylvia had already thought of that. Wright's comment confirmed the decision for her. "I think you're probably right about that."

Agent Wright opened a door with a sign on it that read *Interview 1*. "Right this way. Pick the seat that would make you feel the most comfortable, Patrick."

Patrick entered the room and chose the chair furthest from the door. Sylvia sat two chairs down and Agent Wright sat across from Sylvia. The room only had one dim lamp turned on in a corner. With the door closed, she couldn't hear anything from the hall or surrounding offices.

"Are you ready to begin, Patrick?" Agent Wright opened a notebook and pulled a pen from his shirt pocket. Leaning back in his chair, he crossed one leg over the other.

Patrick mimicked the position except he also cradled his injured arm across his chest. "As ready as I can be, not knowing anything."

"Okay, then, close your eyes and clear your mind. Focus only on the sound of my voice. As soon as you are comfortable, allow yourself to return to the first thing you do remember. What is that thing, Patrick?"

"A gun pointed at me."

"Can you see who is holding it?"

Patrick shook his head slowly. "Not really. I can smell him though."

Agent Wright made a notation on his paper. "What do you mean, you can smell him?"

"His cologne. It's familiar, although I can't quite place it."

"Does it remind you of anything? Or maybe someone?"

Patrick wrinkled his nose as though he were actually smelling the cologne. "It does. But, I have no idea what. I just know I've smelled it before."

"Can you remember anything about the shooter?" Wright asked.

Patrick squeezed his eyes tight. "He's wearing some kind of gloves. Black ones."

Mack carried black leather gloves in his jacket. She carried the black plastic ones for use at crime scenes. The shooter could have had either one on.

"Were they leather? Or maybe plastic? Like hospital gloves?" Sylvia asked.

"I'm not sure what they were made of. All I can see is the color," Patrick said.

"Do you hear any other sounds?" Agent Wright

asked.

"Traffic. I can hear traffic. Horns honking. And music. I think I hear music. Like a band or something."

"That's great, Patrick." Sylvia watched as Agent Wright jotted a few more notes down. "Let's try to back up a little now. How did you end up in the alley in the first place?"

Patrick squeezed his eyes tight again and clenched his fist. "All I remember is walking down the sidewalk. I don't know where I was headed or where I'd come from. Just that I had been walking for a few minutes."

Agent Wright nodded and wrote down a couple more things. "Do you remember seeing anything interesting? Or maybe unusual enough that it caught your attention?

Patrick sniffed. "I smell pizza. And there's one of those old-time photo places. It wasn't open but I think I might have stopped to look in the window?"

"That's very helpful, Patrick."

"How?" he asked, not sounding the least bit convinced.

"It will help us figure out where you might have been coming from." Sylvia hadn't meant to say anything but the words just tumbled right out. She clapped a hand over her mouth.

Agent Wright nodded. "It's okay. I was going to

say the same thing. Patrick? Do you see anything else?"

Patrick shook his head. "No. That's it. I'm sorry." He banged a fist on the arm of the chair. "I can't remember anything else!"

"It's okay." Agent Wright patted the top of his arm. "You remembered a lot more than yesterday. Your memory is coming back a little at a time."

Patrick jumped up out of the chair and paced the room. "Yeah, at this rate, it might be back by the time I'm fifty. Of course, I have no idea when that is since I don't even know who I am."

"Look," Sylvia pointed to Agent Wright's notebook. "You remembered smells, colors, sounds, places. Those are huge details."

"I'm tired. I want to go home. Hell, I want to know *where* home is." Patrick ran his hand through his hair.

Sylvia stepped in front of him and took his hands in hers. "I know how frustrating this is for you. We're all doing everything we can to figure it out but there's nothing. No missing person reports or anything that can even point us in the right direction. The best clues we have just came from you."

Patrick leaned against the wall and sighed. Sylvia looked at him expectantly, like he should just be happy he'd remembered some disgusting cologne and a pizza place. Her hands felt warm and comfortable like they were always meant to hold his.

Agent Wright stepped forward. Sylvia stepped back, letting go. "I know it's hard to accept, but you have made progress today."

"If you say so." He dropped into a chair, wincing when his injury hit the seat back.

A knock on the door interrupted the tension.

"Come in!" Agent Wright called.

An older woman, with shoulder length hair and bright red lipstick, opened the door and stepped in to the room. "Excuse me for interrupting, but I have those phone numbers and addresses you asked for. The Waterside Inn has a double occupancy room open. I took the liberty of reserving it. I can cancel if you prefer one of the other places." She handed the paper to Sylvia.

"Thank you. I appreciate you making those arrangements."

She gave them a bright smile. "You're so welcome. Y'all stay safe now, ya hear?"

The woman left, closing the door behind her.

"You'll like that place," Agent Wright said. "It's not far from here. All the rooms face the water and the security is top notch too. A buddy of mine helped them wire the place when it was being built. Even a ghost can't get past the cameras."

"After our little impromptu visitor this morning,

we could use some super security."

Patrick stood up once more. "Yeah, if you all don't mind, I'd like to live long enough to find out my last name."

Agent Wright picked up his notepad and tucked it under his arm. "I can have a car take you over. Leave yours here so whoever is after you won't see it parked near the hotel."

Sylvia nodded. "That would be great. We need to get our gear out of the trunk first."

"You two just relax here then and I'll find a driver for you." Agent Wright walked out of the room, closing the door behind him.

"I don't know how much more of this I can take and stay sane," Patrick said, breaking the heavy silence of the room.

"When we get to the new place, I'm going to send this information and your photo to the local detectives working the case. They may be able to retrace your steps if you interacted with other people."

He could see how passionate Sylvia was about her job. There was also a hint of something else. Regret, maybe. Regret that she wasn't still a police officer, chasing down the bad guys. He'd seen the sheer thrill in her eyes when she'd been out running the shooter. He got the feeling Sylvia thrived on adrenaline and lived to solve mysteries like his. The more dangerous the better.

"This is fun for you, isn't it?" He reached up and

pushed a wave of hair behind her ears.

She looked down at the floor. "I wouldn't say *fun*, necessarily." Sylvia looked up at him. "Okay, maybe it is a little fun."

The door opened and Agent Wright returned. "This is Agent Trainee Johnson. She's going to take you to the hotel."

Agent Johnson motioned out the door. "If you're ready to go?"

Patrick and Sylvia followed her to the car, chit chatting about weather and other mundane things. They made a quick stop at Sylvia's vehicle to grab their little bit of belongings and thirty minutes later they were checked in and settled in to their new room.

Sylvia flopped down on one of the beds. "Ah, it feels good to lay down."

"This bed is better than the last one. At least I can't feel every spring poking into my back and the support level seems decent." Patrick grabbed the remote control and turned on the television. "Is there anything on besides talk shows and soap operas during the day?"

Sylvia rolled on to her stomach and looked at him. "I have no idea, I don't own a television."

Patrick's mouth fell open in horror. "You. Don't. Own. A. Television? I don't know a damn thing about my life at the moment but I am fairly certain I own multiple T.V.'s."

She laughed. "Okay, so I have a television. I just rarely turn it on. I'm not home much and honestly I do most show watching on my laptop."

He tossed her the little black box. "I'm gonna hit the bathroom. While I'm gone you pick out something to watch."

"But I don't want to!" she called after him as he closed the bathroom door.

He stuck his head back out in to the main room. "We're going to be here awhile, you might as well get used to talk shows."

"Fiiiiinnnneeee," Sylvia whined as he closed the door.

While washing his hands a few minutes later, Sylvia started yelling for him. "Patrick! *Patrick!* Get out here, *now!* You gotta see this!"

He yanked open the door and stepped into the room. "What is the big—Holy crap! Is that me? That's me!"

Plastered across the television screen was a picture of him, wearing a plastic crown. The subtitle read, "Visit Patrick, the Prince of Sleep and you'll get the sleep of your dreams."

"Prince Patrick!" Sylvia jumped off the bed, waving the remote around. "It makes sense now!"

He shook his head, trying to clear the confusion away. "I'm Patrick Everett. My parents are Mark and Andrea Everett and we have a family owned furniture business just outside of Raleigh. I was here for a bachelor party weekend with my two buddies."

Sylvia hit the mute button on the remote. "If you're some famous dude, why hasn't anyone filed a missing person's report?"

"Because—my name is Hairston Patrick Everett." He held up a hand when Sylvia looked like she wanted to comment. "Don't say it—now you know why I go by Patrick. Hairston is my mother's maiden name. My parents would have used my full name and the guys probably thought I left town."

Sylvia dropped back on the bed. "I can't believe you're famous. How did I not know this?"

"You said you don't watch television. There's no way you would know. I mean, unless you'd seen the billboards all over North Carolina or listened to any local radio station."

Sylvia chuckled. "You're a prince—ish. Who hates to sleep on uncomfortable beds. And I'm a *peace* offi-cer. We're the *Prince—ish and the Peace*! You know, like *The Princess and the Pea*?"

He grinned and shook his head. "You're kinda crazy, you know that?"

She jumped back up and wrapped her arms around Patrick, resting her cheek against his chest, reveling in the simple contact. She'd been a lot lone-lier than she'd ever thought. "I'm so glad your memory came back. Does that sound teenage girl with a crush on a celebrity—ish?"

"Very much so." He leaned down and pressed a kiss to the top of her hair. "Know what else I remember?"

Sylvia tilted her head to look up at him, her green eyes shining. "What?"

"I'm not married and I definitely don't have a girlfriend."

"There's still the little issue of professional conduct and all that. I never should have let things progress last night at all."

He placed his hand on her shoulder and looked into those amazing pools of emerald where Sylvia hung her heart and then kissed her forehead lightly. "As soon as this case is wrapped up, we are going on a real date."

She nodded. "I'd definitely be on board with that. It's been a long time though, I might be out of practice."

"We will figure it out together."

Those green eyes lit up with a hint of excitement. "Do you remember where you live?"

He smiled. "I do. Downtown Raleigh, North Carolina. In fact, I should call my parents."

Her expression changed to one of concern. God, he loved watching the color in her eyes change. "You can't! Not yet. I don't want word to get out you remember anything. If someone is still after you, they will step up their game."

Patrick frowned. "I suppose you are right."

She squeezed his hand lightly. "Very soon."

He needed to speed the process up so they could stop being witness and Marshal. Now that he knew who he was, he wanted to get to know everything—and every inch of Sylvia Fairfax, the woman behind the badge. "I want to go back to that alley one more time. There's still some missing details and I think it would help to be there; trigger my brain some to fill in the blanks."

"Yeah, that would help, I bet." She pulled her cell phone from her pocket and dialed a number. "I just have to let my boss know your identity and that your memory is coming back. Then I'll arrange us a ride to the beach."

Patrick watched as Sylvia sent her texts and arranged them an *Uber* pick up. The seriousness of her job seemed so at odds with the way her eyes opened straight in to her soul. Sylvia felt everything very deeply, even if she appeared cool as a cucumber on the outside. That much he'd already learned about the woman that had slowly begun to take over his heart.

"Okay. The car should be here in five minutes. You ready to solve this case?" Sylvia's excitement made her cheeks pink and those amazing eyes sparkle.

Patrick stood up from the chair he'd been sitting in. "Let's do this."

CHAPTER EIGHT

Sylvia sent a quick text to Mack, updating him on the progress they'd made since he'd left that morning. Even though he retired in less than a week, she knew her partner would be interested.

At least she'd thought so. When no reply came by the time the car pulled up to their destination, Sylvia dropped her phone in her pocket with the sound on so she'd hear if he responded.

"You good?" Patrick sat beside her, fiddling with a thread at the hem of his shirt

"Yup." He opened the door and stepped out of the car. Sylvia followed him. She'd decided to let Patrick take the lead, to see if that helped his memory.

He walked over to the trash dumpster where they'd found him that night. A dark stain still colored the concrete.

"That was a lot of blood." Patrick pressed the toe

of his shoe to the stain. "How did I ever survive that?"

"Scientifically, there may be several reasons. The bullet missed a major artery, for one. It was also really cold and the low temperatures could slow blood flow." Sylvia pointed to the ground where they'd found the other body. That had been a carotid artery shot, every pump of his heart had been deadly after the bullet pierced his neck. The killer knew what he was doing with that one. "Look at that stain. Now that's a lot of blood."

Patrick shrugged. "I guess so."

"Do you remember anything new?" Sylvia didn't want to prod too much but the temperatures were dropping quickly.

"Actually, I do. As soon as we pulled up, I remembered why I'd come to Virginia Beach in the first place."

Sylvia rubbed her hands together to create a little warmth. "Really?"

He nodded. "My best friend from childhood is getting married this month. We were here for a bachelor's only weekend with his brother."

Sylvia narrowed her eyes as she considered this. "You said that earlier. But, you were alone."

"I know. I left the bar we'd been at because my friend is a pig and I didn't want to be a part of his games."

"Ah, cheated on the fiancée, did he?"

Patrick shrugged. "I assume so. I told them I had to make a call, walked out, and next thing I know I hear a man begging for his life. Said he wouldn't testify and that he'd escaped so he wouldn't have to."

"That's really good, Patrick. That helps us a lot."

"Do you smell that?" he asked, looking around.

Sylvia frowned and sniffed the air. "What is it? I don't smell anything."

"It's that same smelly cologne that the killer wore. I'd know that stink anywhere."

A soft click, as someone pulled back the hammer on a revolver, sounded behind them. At the same time Sylvia also recognized the heavy scent of a very familiar aftershave.

She spun to face the person aiming a gun at them. "Mack! What are you doing?"

Mack glared at them, a snarl of a smile twisting his lips. "Tying up some loose ends. Not sure why you didn't die the other night Prince Patrick but I'm here to rewrite the ending of the fairy tale."

"Mack!" Sylvia reached for the gun but Mack jerked his hand out of the way.

"Let me do this, Syl. I'll keep you out of it if you can just keep your mouth shut."

"I can't let you kill a witness!" She stepped between Mack and Patrick.

Mack waved the gun, motioning her to move but Sylvia stayed put. "I already have. If this numb nut hadn't shown up and tried to play hero, we'd have both been long gone from here and no one would have known."

"You're retiring in a few days! Why risk murdering our own witness?" Sylvia looked angry but Patrick saw the hurt dark in her eyes.

"You think my government retirement is gonna be enough? One good payoff from the Carisi family and Susan and I could live well in our golden years. I gotta think about my family. Now stop talking. Both of you face the wall and get down on your knees."

"Mack—"

"Shut up already, Fairfax, and just do as you're told for once in your ridiculous life!" Mack poked her shoulder blade with the barrel of his revolver. "And you, prince boy, make sure you die this time."

"Drop the gun, McCoy!"

"What?" Mack spun, the revolver still in his hand. "What are *you* doing here?"

Sylvia turned around to the self-satisfied smirk of Agent Wright of the FBI. She let out a long breath of air. "Right on time."

Wright motioned to a couple of guys to take Mack into custody. Her former partner set the revolver on the ground and lifted his hands.

Patrick looked from her to the men and back again. "I don't get it. How did they end up here?"

"I texted him and asked him to meet us here. I thought he might be helpful if you hit a mental block."

Patrick wrapped his arms around her and pulled her to his chest. "Do you have any idea how amazing you are?"

Sylvia shrugged. "Kinda. But you can tell me anytime you want."

"What if I show you?" He leaned in and Sylvia met him halfway, pressing her lips to his.

"All right, you two. We're still technically on the clock." Agent Wright tapped an imaginary watch on his wrist. "We need to let the locals know and get everyone together for a big debriefing. Statements from everyone!" Wright laughed. "I'll take this guy. You two catch a ride with one of my agents. Patrick has to give a statement about what happened that night. I assume your memory has returned?"

Patrick nodded. "One hundred percent and counting."

"Excellent! Let's get this show on the road then."

<hr>

He hung up the receiver of the phone he'd been directed to, replacing it in the cradle, his mother's joy still fresh in his ears.

"Everything okay?" Sylvia asked.

He smiled, wanting desperately to take her in his arms. "Yeah. It is now. When Derek and Devin had returned to Raleigh without me, my parents filed a missing person's report with the Virginia Beach

Police Department. Except they used my first name, Hairston, instead of Patrick, my middle name and the one I use. Just like I thought."

Sylvia nodded. "No wonder we couldn't find anything."

"Mom is making me all my favorite foods tomorrow for dinner. She wanted me to come straight home tonight but I told her I wanted a good-night's rest before the long drive. You know, my banged-up head and all." He tapped his temple with the finger of his uninjured arm. "Plus, the room at the inn is already paid for—"

A wide smiled spread across Sylvia's lips as her eyes gleamed with humor. "And you thought you might want to try out yet another mattress that isn't going to be good enough?"

"Oh, it will be good enough." He winked. "I won't even notice if its lumpy, I promise."

"I thought you wanted to go on a real date, get to know each other?" Sylvia pouted. "I'm not interested in a one night stand."

Patrick glanced around the room then bent to whisper in her ear. "You don't have to worry about that. One night will never be enough."

He watched, with a pleased smile, the deep flush that filled her fair skin. She batted her eye lashes at him. "Why, Prince Patrick, are you looking for a happy ending to this story?"

"Isn't that how it's supposed to go? The prince

falls in love and they live happily ever after in a castle?"

She stepped in close, running her fingertips over the fabric of his shirt. "Do you have a castle?"

He leaned in and nibbled her earlobe lightly. "More like a fifth floor condo but it has a balcony, does that count?"

Sylvia reached behind her and opened a door to a supply closet. Stepping back, she pulled him with her. Once the door closed, she pressed her body against his until he leaned against the door. "I think it counts just fine." Sliding her hands up over his chest, careful to avoid his bandages, Sylvia looked up at him. Even in the dark, her green eyes glowed, like a cat's eyes.

Pressing a line of kisses from her temple to the corner of her mouth, Patrick parted his lips and whispered. "Is it time for the prince to kiss his princess?"

Instead of answering, she stood up on tiptoe and kissed him. The moment her lips touched his, Patrick knew he'd found his happily ever after.

Science teacher by day, writer and mom by night, Carolyn LaRoche lives near the ocean with her husband, two boys, rescue puppy and two cats. She loves baseball, books, food videos and trying new recipes. The beach is her happy place and snow has become her arch enemy after years of living in New England.

Visit her online at:

www.ingramcontent.com/pod-product-compliance
Lightning Source LLC
Chambersburg PA
CBHW022156150726
47992CB00002B/812